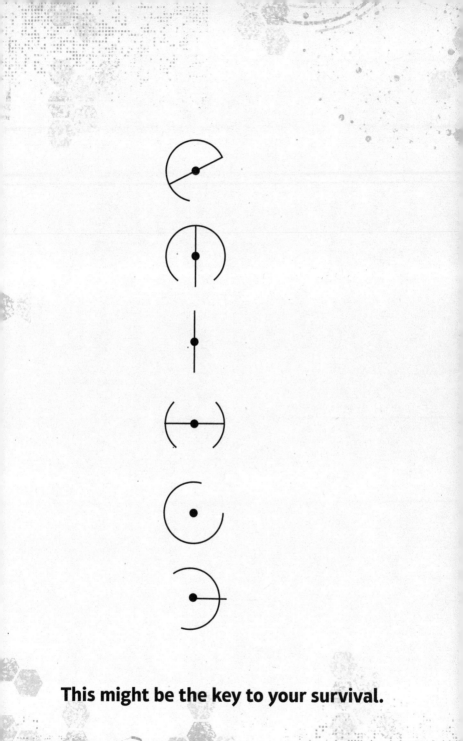

This might be the key to your survival.

JUNE 13, 2018

SCOTT WESTERFELD

X

SCHOLASTIC INC.

Library of Congress Control Number Available

ISBN 978-0-545-91677-6

10 9 8 7 6 5 4 3 2 1   17 18 19 20 21

Book design by Abby Dening

First edition, January 2017

Printed in the U.S.A.   23

Scholastic US: 557 Broadway · New York, NY 10012
Scholastic Canada: 604 King Street West · Toronto, ON M5V 1E1
Scholastic New Zealand Limited: Private Bag 94407 · Greenmount, Manukau 2141
Scholastic UK Ltd.: Euston House · 24 Eversholt Street · London NW1 1DB

To everyone who builds,
designs, and makes

TRANSCRIPT, AERO HORIZON FLIGHT 16

RETRIEVED FROM AIR TRAFFIC CONTROL RECORDINGS, FAIRBANKS, ALASKA.

FAI = Sam Tennison, Fairbanks Air Traffic Control
Captain Frank Benoit, AH16
First Officer Alexis Card, AH16
Flight Attendant Pete Meriwether, AH16

- -

21:13:42.7

>**FAI:** Aero Horizon 16, things are looking bumpy ahead of you.
>
>**CAPTAIN:** We see it. How deep?
>
>**FAI:** You should be through in two minutes.
>
>**CAPTAIN:** Thanks, Fairbanks.
>
>**FAI:** No problem.
>
>**FIRST OFFICER:** Pete, can you sit them down back there?
>
>**FLIGHT ATTENDANT (INTERCOM):** Us too?
>
>(pause)
>
>**FIRST OFFICER:** Everyone.

21:15:24.3

>**CAPTAIN:** Are you seeing this?
>
>**FIRST OFFICER:** (unintelligible) ... flash of lightning?
>
>**CAPTAIN:** But it's just sitting there.
>
>**FIRST OFFICER:** We've got an electrical—
>
>**CAPTAIN:** Losing everything!

FIRST OFFICER: Battery kicking in.

CAPTAIN: Okay. Okay. Instruments are back.

FIRST OFFICER: What WAS that?

CAPTAIN: I'm taking us lower. We need to get under this.

21:15:50.1

(alarm)

FIRST OFFICER: Bird strike. We have bird strike.

CAPTAIN: At 28,000 feet? There's no birds up—

FIRST OFFICER: On engine three. Flame condition.

CAPTAIN: Shut it down.

FIRST OFFICER: I'm trying.

FAI: The status of your aircraft, please.

FIRST OFFICER: We have fire in number three. Won't shut down. Losing speed ...

(stall alarm)

(auto-pilot disengage alarm)

CAPTAIN: We are in manual. Descending.

FIRST OFFICER: Okay.

CAPTAIN: I have the controls.

FIRST OFFICER: Smoke in the cockpit.

(multiple alarms)

FAI: Horizon 16, we have an emergency inbound runway available.

CAPTAIN: We're unable.

FLIGHT ATTENDANT (INTERCOM): We have smoke in the cabin.

FIRST OFFICER: Right ahead! Another one!

FAI: I'm sorry. Say again?

CAPTAIN: We—What IS that?

(sound of metal tearing)

FIRST OFFICER: It's in here with us! It's in here with—

(sound of rushing air)

CAPTAIN: She's (unintelligible) gone.

(sound of tearing metal, rushing air)

21:16:14.2

FAI: Horizon 16, radar contact is lost.

(unintelligible)

FAI: Horizon 16, are you still on?

(rushing air)

FAI: Horizon 16?

(radio contact lost)

— —

End of transcript. Cause of crash as yet undetermined.

No black box found. No wreckage found.

No survivors found.

EIGHT HOURS
EARLIER

Javi

ext question," Molly said. "How many miles of wire are in this airplane?"

"Um, a lot?"

"Put your brain to work, Perez. Estimate!"

Javier Perez sighed. "If I get close, will you stop bugging me with these questions?"

"Nope. You need the distraction." Molly clutched her book of airplane trivia and grinned. "I've got at least fourteen hours' worth. Enough for the whole flight!"

"*You* wanted to sit by her!" Anna said from the row behind, and Oliver laughed beside her.

Javi groaned, wishing the plane would take off so he could lean back and pretend to sleep.

Telling Molly that he was afraid of flying had been a terrible idea. Because that made it her job, as team leader, to distract him—with engineering problems, of course. At Robotics Club every afternoon, Molly always talked while she worked, explaining what she was doing, challenging others to do the same. For her, making robots wasn't just a hobby, it was a *conversation*.

The funny thing was, the distraction was actually working. Once Javi's brain had latched onto her question, the plane became more than a huge unknown carrying him away from home for the first time ever. Now it was an engineering problem.

How many miles of wire? Javi thought.

The four members of Team Killbot, along with their adviser, Mr. Keating, were sitting in economy. Brooklyn Science and Tech had lots of rich people who donated money to the school, and when the team had qualified for the Robot Soccer World Championships, some millionaire had stepped up to pay travel costs.

But first class to Japan for five people? Nobody had *that* much money to give away.

Even so, this was what Mr. Keating called "fancy economy," designed for fourteen-hour flights. Javi's seat was surrounded by buttons and lights and a video screen. All of which were connected to wires, right?

He'd already tested the buttons on his armrest. They controlled the angle of his seat, a reading light, the screen. There was a button for summoning a flight attendant, and a rocker switch with volume symbols. There was even a little remote control for games (which also seemed to be a phone, in case you needed to call someone from halfway across the Arctic Circle).

Javi found himself wanting to strip it all down, to see those wires, motors, and gears out in the open. He'd been taking things apart as long as he could remember, starting when his mother had let him take apart her busted microwave when he was five years old.

He imagined the wires under the cabin floor, snaking up and around the curves of the chair. And another bright web above him, bringing power to all those lights and air blowers in the ceiling—

"Conjectures?" Molly prompted. "Conclusions?"

Javi's brain buzzed. Each seat would need at least a hundred feet of wire, and there were about five hundred people on the plane. That was *ten miles* right there, on top of the ailerons and engines, the cockpit crammed with gauges, the extra wires needed for the huge business class seats a few rows ahead.

Too much to calculate, so he multiplied his first guess by ten.

"In the whole plane, maybe a hundred miles of wire?"

"Not too bad." Molly waved her book. "But it's more like *three* hundred. A technical tour de force!"

"Okay, wow," Javi said, though amazement was the surest route to more trivia questions. "It seems like a waste, using a machine this complicated to fly our dinky little robots to Tokyo."

"The Killbots are *not* dinky," Molly said. "They're the reigning US champions of robot soccer, junior division!"

Javi shrugged. "May I remind you that the other team's robots got broken in shipping? We lucked into this."

"We would've won anyway." Molly's expression dared him to argue.

Javi wasn't sure. He'd seen videos of the robots built by the unlucky finalists from New Mexico—scuttling four-legged scorpions that whacked the soccer ball with their tails. In stark contrast, the Brooklyn Killbots were toasters on wheels. Mindless bullies that swarmed the ball, knocking other players out their way.

"Like how five-year-olds play soccer," one of the judges had muttered in the semifinals.

And there were, what, maybe twenty feet of wire in each Killbot?

Not exactly a technical tour de force.

Last night, Javi's whole family had gathered for a send-off dinner: uncles, aunts, and cousins all telling him how proud they were. His mother had told stories of him helping on her superintendent rounds when he was little, fixing locks and faucets at age seven. But for the whole dinner he'd felt like a fraud.

What kind of engineer was afraid to get on an airplane?

"Next question," Molly said. "How many Aero Horizon flights have ever crashed?"

He stared at her. Was she just trolling him now?

If building robots had taught Javi anything, it was that way too much could go wrong with machines. No matter how carefully he tested them, the Killbots were always doing unpredictable stuff in the middle of a match.

He thought about those three hundred miles of wire in the airplane, the millions of rivets and seals and screws, the engines and tanks full of flammable fuel. All those parts that could break, warp, fail, or explode.

"I'm going to go with . . . two?" he said hopefully.

"Nope," Molly said. "Zero!"

"Really?"

"Yep. No crashes in the whole fleet, in forty years."

"Huh." Javi felt a relieved smile reach his lips, and his irritation with Molly faded. Even when she was trolling him, she always had a plan. "Thanks."

She shrugged, as if to say that his fears were forgotten. "Just enjoy the flight, Perez. We're going to win for real this time."

Javi gave her a fist to bump. "Team Killbot!"

Mr. Keating leaned forward from the row behind. "Um, guys. Maybe no more discussion of airplane crashes?"

"Actually," Molly said, "we were discussing the total *absence* of airplane crashes."

"Still," Mr. Keating said firmly. "Some people are nervous about flying."

"Not us engineers." Molly smiled at Javi. "Next question . . ."

"*Last* question," Javi pleaded.

Molly looked like she was about to argue, but then a *ping* went through the cabin, and a voice announced that the doors were closing.

Javi swallowed. Last night, he had imagined himself jumping up and running off the plane when this moment came. But thanks to Molly's distractions, he was managing to sit here quietly.

"Fire away," he said.

"This is my favorite one." Molly clutched the trivia book close, guarding the answer. "What do flight attendants call it when the oxygen masks drop down?"

Javi frowned. "There's a name for that?"

"It's secret flight attendant slang. Let me give you a hint: The oxygen sensor gets tripped, right? And suddenly all those rubber masks fall out of the ceiling. Everyone's freaking out, screaming like *animals*. So what do flight attendants call it?"

"Um, a really bad day at work?"

"Nope." Molly gave him a pleased smile. "They call it a 'rubber jungle.' Get it? Because everyone goes primal, and there's all those masks hanging down like vines! And usually it's just an accident, because of a broken sensor."

Javi tried to smile back at her, but now he was thinking about those hundreds of masks up in the ceiling, each tightly wound in its little compartment, like snakes ready to spring out and start a panic.

Just one more thing that could go wrong.

2

Yoshi

The kids a few rows back were talking about airplane crashes again.

Yoshi Kimura could hear the girl closest to him even over the announcements. She kept sharing *fascinating* technical details about the plane. This was the problem with his mom buying his ticket so late. He'd been stuck only a few rows from the economy section—all those people who thought sitting in a tin can for fourteen hours was exciting.

Yoshi couldn't wait for the plane to take off, for the roar of its engines to drown out everyone's voices and leave him with his own glum thoughts.

For the hundredth time, he wondered what awaited him at the end of this flight. His father had promised a punishment as epic as it was long-delayed, but had left the details to Yoshi's imagination.

An attendant appeared and said in careful English, "Would you like something to drink before takeoff, sir?"

"Mizu, onegaishimasu," Yoshi replied, and was pleased when she looked surprised. Japanese people always thought he looked too Western—too much like a *hafu*—to speak in a flawless accent. But he'd lived his first ten years in Tokyo, before Mom had given up and moved back to New York.

The attendant bowed, slipped away, and returned with a tiny bottle of water. Yoshi drained it in one gulp, but his throat stayed dry.

The weird thing was, he'd been much calmer on his way here to New York, nine months ago. Even with a priceless four-hundred-year-old sword in his baggage—stolen from his own father—he hadn't been worried.

Of course, back then he hadn't known he was breaking the law just by taking the family katana out of Japan. His father had always told Yoshi that it would be his one day but had never mentioned that it was an official Cultural Property, a national treasure too precious to leave the country.

The sword was in the hold of the airplane now, safely sheathed and in its travel case. And insured for four hundred thousand dollars, an amount that was somehow more impressive than words like *Cultural Property*.

On the phone yesterday, Yoshi had asked his father what would happen if Japanese customs took a close look at it. Could they arrest him for bringing it *back into* the country?

"You should have thought of that before you stole it" was all Father would say. Yoshi hadn't pointed out that the whole reason for taking the sword was so he'd never have to go back to Japan again.

But that plan hadn't exactly worked, had it?

The announcements finally ended, and soon the plane was rumbling down the runway, gaining speed, and lifting into the air. It leaned into an unhurried turn as it climbed, slicing through the sky like a vast, graceful blade.

When at last it reached straight and level flight, Yoshi reclined his seat all the way, until it was as flat as a bed. He curled up under the blanket, wrapped in noise-canceling headphones, staring at a tablet full of anime.

He had to binge-watch everything now. His father was almost certainly going to take his screens away when he got to Tokyo. No computers, phones, or TV for a month had been Yoshi's punishment for failing a calligraphy test at age nine.

Whatever his father had in mind now would be much worse than that and would last all summer. Which meant disappearing from his New York friends' lives. By September, everyone would've moved on to new shows, new music, new manga. And Yoshi would be forgotten. He'd be a foreign kid, starting all over again, just like three years ago when he'd first arrived.

He would always be foreign, it seemed, always on the wrong side of the Pacific Ocean.

The flight attendant came by and lightly touched his

shoulder, probably to ask about dinner. Yoshi just shook his head, retreating further under the covers. He didn't want her to see that his eyes were glistening.

He found himself hoping that the airplane never made it to Japan.

3

Molly

The white stretched out beneath Molly Davis in endless sheets.

In some places the snow lay in waves, like sand dunes carved smooth by the wind. In others, ice rose up from colliding floes in jagged, broken spires. The sun was just above the horizon and cast long shadows across rippling white.

Molly shivered, looking at all that ice. According to the flight tracker map on her video screen, the plane was well above the Arctic Circle now.

No cities. No roads. She hadn't seen anything but arctic white in ages.

Which raised an interesting question. If Javi's worst fears came true and the plane crashed, would the passengers freeze to death before help arrived?

Molly looked around the cabin. It was June, so nobody was wearing anything heavier than a sweater. And those flimsy airplane blankets wouldn't even keep you warm in a movie theater.

Maybe you could make survival tents out of the life rafts pictured on the safety card. Or keep yourself warm with jet fuel. Was there a way to burn it steadily? Or would you just blow yourself up, along with what remained of the plane?

She turned from the window to ask Javi for help with the problem, but he was still asleep.

That was annoying. He'd been jittering like a bag of windup teeth all morning, but now that Molly was bored he was unconscious.

It was better than him sulking, she supposed. Ever since Team Killbot had won the championship by default, he'd acted like they weren't really winners. Like they *deserved* for things to go wrong in Tokyo. Well, the other finalists' bad luck wasn't Team Killbot's fault.

That's what you got for making fragile robots. You could ship the Killbots a thousand miles in the back of a bouncy UPS truck, and they'd probably work just fine. They were simple. And they kicked butt.

That was how good engineers built things.

Molly looked back at Oliver and Anna, hoping that one of them was awake. Nope, they were asleep, too. Even Mr. Keating was snoring.

Turned out that fourteen hours was a *long* time. Molly hated having no one to talk to. At home when Mom got quiet,

Molly sometimes even talked to herself, answering her own questions. Anything was better than silence.

She looked down at the ice and shivered again.

Javi let out a sputtery snore, and Molly wondered if she should get some sleep, too. Team Killbot's first match was the day after they landed, and she had no idea what jet lag felt like. Javi wasn't the only kid at Brooklyn Science and Tech who'd never flown before.

She shut the window shade against the endless white and settled back into her seat. The airplane pillow smelled weird, so she dropped it on the floor and scrunched up her sweater.

With the steady roar of the plane in her ears, Molly could almost imagine falling asleep . . .

In her dream, snow still rolled beneath the airplane, endless and empty.

Molly could see everything now, not only through her little window, but in all directions. She saw the ice floes stirred by the ocean beneath them, pushed by the winds spinning around the globe. From up here, the forces that shaped the ice all made so much *sense*, like when she grasped a solution to an engineering problem.

But there was something ahead that didn't make any sense at all. Out there in the snow, a hundred miles away, something was waiting. Something that reminded Molly of her mother—lonely, angry at fate, and a little confused.

But it knew what it wanted.

It reached out, grasping with lines of pure force . . .

. . . for the airplane.

A jolt went through Molly's body, along with a blazing white in her mind as bright as the snow outside.

The thing out there in the ice, its claws were *inside* the plane now—slicing and cutting along the seams, setting those hundreds of miles of wire aflame, bending the course of the shuddering aircraft by sheer force of will.

Then the blaze of its attention turned from the shell of metal and saw *her*, Molly Davis. It reached straight into her mind, lighting up her brain. Like it wanted to know her . . .

Molly awoke gasping from the dream, but out here in the real world, things were just as bewildering. The cabin lights pulsed and flickered, and the plane was shuddering beneath her. Smoke filled the air.

"No way." She turned to Javi. "Am I awake?"

"I sure am." His face was pale.

One in ten million, Molly thought. Those were the odds of a jetliner going down, according to her trivia book. She was about to say it out loud when the shriek of an alarm filled the cabin, and five hundred oxygen masks suddenly tumbled from the ceiling. They danced and swung with the rocking of the airplane, like a chorus of horrible puppets flailing among the light and smoke and noise.

It was a rubber jungle, and everybody started screaming.

Anna

An oxygen mask jumped and bounced like a living thing in front of Anna Klimek's face. She grabbed for it, her mind racing, trying to remember what to do next.

To start the flow of oxygen, pull it toward yourself.

Oxygen sounded like a good thing. Anna pulled the mask against her mouth and took a deep breath. It smelled like antiseptic and rubber, which was better than the acrid smoke that had woken her up. Her eyes stung and she could barely see. She held the mask against her face with one hand.

Next to Anna, Mr. Keating was shouting something, but she couldn't understand him over the squeal of the alarms. The plane bucked beneath her, sending a jolt up her spine.

She turned to Oliver. He was gripping his armrests and his

mouth was open in a scream she couldn't hear. With her free hand, she grabbed at his oxygen mask and pushed it into his face. He stared at it for a moment like he didn't recognize it, but finally took it and held it to his mouth.

His eyes were bright with tears, and Anna tried to smile, to reassure him. But her face felt frozen, disconnected from her mind.

What was she supposed to do now? She replayed the safety announcements in her mind. Something about a crash position . . .

Right. This was really happening—the plane was crashing.

Something clicked inside Anna, and suddenly her fear was gone, replaced by questions.

Does hitting the ground hurt? Or is it over too fast to feel anything?

She almost found it comforting, when this cold, emotion-less part of her brain took over in emergencies.

But her panic was rekindled by what happened next.

A tearing sound filled the plane, a metal shriek from directly overhead—the ceiling splitting open. The great spine of overhead luggage compartments and lights and little air blowers lifted away, shattering into a million pieces of beige plastic as it rose. The oxygen mask was yanked free from her hand and went spinning into the sudden wind.

"No way," she breathed.

Through the huge hole, a sudden white sky shone down on Anna, hard sunlight and snow-filled air. The wind was freez-ing, blustering at hundreds of miles an hour, forcing her smoke-stung eyes into a squint. Her ears popped so hard her whole head felt like it was bursting.

The gale in the cabin reached into the seat-back pockets to seize magazines and safety cards and boarding passes, churning them into a blizzard of paper that slapped at her face and hands. But a moment later all that debris had fluttered up and away. Nothing was left but the snapped wires and shreds of plastic at the edges of the torn roof, trembling madly in the wind.

The oddly rational part of Anna's brain wondered, *How are we still flying?*

It seemed like the entire airplane should just surrender and fold up around her, like something made of tinfoil. But somehow it was still slicing through the freezing air in a straight course, as if guided by a giant hand.

And now something even weirder was happening—an electrical storm shot through the cabin, a hundred-legged spider made of lightning that skittered from seat to seat.

When it reached Anna, a buzzing filled her mind, along with pain as bright as the white sky. Her eyes slammed shut, but she couldn't keep it out—the lightning crawled through her head, rummaging and pillaging.

It felt like it was *testing* her, running a thousand little logic problems through her mind. For a moment Anna's brain almost seized up, but then the cold, unpanicked part of her took over, weirdly delighted to play along.

When the lightning finally passed, it left her mind feeling scoured and bruised.

She blinked her eyes and turned to Mr. Keating. "What was *that*?"

But he wasn't there. Not even his *seat* was there, just a jagged hole in the floor of the cabin.

"Wait—" Anna started to say.

The dazzling light swept past her again and wrapped itself around the man across the aisle. His whole body went into spasms, and from his mouth erupted a shriek that Anna could hear even over the roaring winds.

The man's seat began to shudder, to bend and deform beneath him. Then all at once it tore itself from the cabin floor and lifted up, and both seat and man were flung out through the ceiling into the blinding white sky.

"No," Anna squeezed out through clenched teeth. "This is a dream."

It was a relief, the sudden certainty that *this could not be happening.*

The lightning moved on down the line, and Anna slammed closed her eyes against the blinding unreality of it. She tried to shut out the sounds of screams and tearing metal, the buffeting air that was too cold to breathe.

She shut out everything. Putting her fists against her mouth, she screamed into them, wishing this all away. But the light and noise and freezing cold refused to fade.

When Anna opened her eyes again, the cabin had almost been stripped bare of seats. But Javi and Molly were still there in front, and Oliver beside her.

The weird lightning was gone, but the wind was just as wild.

For a moment, Anna's eyes caught something through the cracked plastic of her window. A huge wall shimmered past, shining like a mirror, as if the sky was turning solid around them.

But then white mist filled her window, and the sky above muddled into cloud. The freezing air grew damp.

A *crack* came from beneath her. Then a thousand shrieks shivered through the plane—something was scraping along the bottom.

Just in time, Anna remembered the announcement about crash positions and leaned her elbows against the back of Javi's seat. The plane jolted sickeningly as it hit the ground, then rocked from side to side in a long, skidding stop. Snapping and ripping sounds filled her ears along the way.

Finally, the airplane came to rest, the cabin floor tipped at a funhouse angle. She eased back against her seat and stared up through the torn roof.

The sky was laced with leaves and branches.

This last bit of weirdness somehow switched off the remaining shreds of panic inside Anna. There wasn't room for fear anymore. Suddenly, she was watching everything from a thousand miles away.

Birds fluttered past, shrieking, upset that this giant metal thing had come crashing down into their forest. And from the depths of her strange calmness, Anna noticed that they didn't sound like any birds she'd ever heard before.

5

Javi

I n the sudden stillness, Javi's ears roared, and the light was blinding. His seat was tilted and something clung to his face, smothering him. When he tried to push it away, it snapped back against his mouth.

Elastic straps. The oxygen mask. Of course.

Javi pulled it off his head and realized that the air hose didn't lead to anything. There was no ceiling above him, just bright sky.

He remembered now—the plane had been torn open from the top.

Javi tried to stand but couldn't. Even pressing down with both hands, he could rise only an inch from his seat . . .

Were his legs broken?

"Seat belt," came Molly's voice.

"Oh, right." Javi unclipped himself and stood. His legs definitely worked, but he wobbled for a moment. Then his eyes finally adjusted, and he saw how tilted the floor of the cabin was. Most of the seats were gone.

Most of the people, too.

He looked around and saw only Molly, Anna, and Oliver. Team Killbot, but no one else.

"Where is everyone?"

Anna started to answer, but Molly cut her off. "We should get outside. In case there's a fire."

Javi sniffed the air. He didn't know what jet fuel smelled like, but he was pretty sure it didn't smell like this—humid and pungent, like a hothouse full of flowers.

He squinted up through the torn roof and saw that the rubber jungle had been replaced by . . . a *real* jungle?

Trees towered over the plane, sprouting reddish ferns and flowers with spiky crimson petals. Screeching birds flittered across the view. The sky was pillowy white, as if the jungle floated in a cloud. And the strangest thing of all—it was *warm*. The air was heavy with moisture, like a Brooklyn midsummer day without a breath of wind.

"Where *is* this?" he breathed.

All four of them stared up at the trees for a long moment. But then Javi's eyes fell again to the jagged stumps where the seats should have been.

It was too much to take in, and the roar in his ears started to build again.

"What's happening?" Oliver said. He was clutching Anna's hand, but she barely seemed to know he was there.

"Why aren't we freezing to death?" she asked.

The rest of Team Killbot looked at Molly, like they usually did when an insolvable problem presented itself.

"I don't know," she said. "We're not going to figure it out in here. Especially if the plane blows up!"

She pointed at the emergency exit.

A tremor of relief went through Javi. Anything was better than standing here, contemplating the missing seats that stretched out like rows of broken teeth around them.

They picked their way across the torn and tilted floor of the cabin. Javi reached the exit first and peered through the little window. The metal trapezoid of the wing was shredded, the flaps and ailerons yanked out by the crash. The shiny metal looked alien amid the jungle's wild shapes and colors.

He glanced at the diagram over the emergency exit, then pulled on the big red handle. The door eased from its frame, and Javi pushed it out. It landed with a *bang* on the wing, sending a shrieking chorus of birds into the air. A hissing sound came from outside—an evacuation slide inflating automatically.

Javi stepped out carefully. Wet red fronds lay scattered across the metal, and the wing had huge dents along its forward edge—it had sliced through trees while skidding to a halt. From out here, Javi could see a path of destruction stretching back along the landing path.

Pieces of wreckage, strewn luggage, broken trees. But no bodies anywhere.

Five hundred people, just . . . gone.

"Javi, keep moving," Molly murmured.

The evacuation slide had taken only seconds to inflate. It was chubby and bright yellow, like something from a bouncy castle. But it worked. A minute later, the four of them were on the ground, which was soft with a thick undergrowth of red vines. The whole jungle seemed tinged with red, and every inch of it was alive. Under the shriek of birds, an insect-like buzz came from the iridescent blurs flitting along the ground.

Team Killbot stood there a moment at the bottom of the slide, silent.

"That doesn't make sense," Molly murmured.

She was staring back at the plane—what was left of it, anyway. There was no tail section, just a jagged tear about forty feet behind the wing. And at the front end, the cockpit gaped open, empty.

"No tail section, no pilots," she said. "But we came down in a straight line, like a controlled crash landing."

"When it should have cartwheeled down," Anna calmly agreed. "We should all be dead."

Oliver's hand dropped from hers as he pulled away.

"What do you *mean*?" he cried. "*None* of this makes sense! We're in the wrong place, and everyone else is missing. We must have gotten knocked out, and everyone else went to get help!"

Javi nodded. Help was coming, of course. Help always arrived after big crashes—search planes and helicopters and ground parties. Airliners constantly updated their position with air traffic control. They didn't just disappear . . .

"But why would *everyone* leave the plane?" Molly asked. "Hundreds of people wouldn't just march off into the jungle!"

"They didn't leave," Anna said. "They were taken."

Molly

Molly stared at Anna.

"Something came into the plane during the crash," Anna said, her voice steady. "Some kind of electricity."

A chill came over Molly. She had seen the lightning moving from seat to seat. She'd thought it was a dream, some kind of brain-fritz caused by panic. But if Anna had seen it, too, maybe it was real.

Molly remembered how the lightning had felt in her head—probing her, testing her, finally accepting her.

Rejecting others.

"It took people," Anna said. "Just lifted them up and—"

"We'll figure that out later," Molly cut in. Oliver wasn't ready to hear this.

She wasn't sure if *any* of them were ready to talk about what had happened to the other passengers, but Oliver was the team mascot, two years younger than the rest of them. His mom hadn't even wanted to sign the permission letter for the trip, until Molly had promised to look out for him.

Now he was staring off into the jungle, as if expecting a rescue party to appear. If he started panicking, everyone else would, too. Including Molly herself.

She needed to distract them, and trivia questions weren't going to cut it.

"First things first: We have to figure out if those engines are about to blow up, okay?"

That got everyone's attention. All eyes turned to the two huge engines on this side's wing. They looked like they'd bashed through a few dozen trees on the way down. Their intakes were stuffed with leaves and shredded bark, even a few bright feathers. The engines steamed in the wet air, creaking and hissing like wet wood on a fire. Molly saw charred metal but no flames.

"I don't smell fuel," Javi said.

Anna nodded. "Something sliced the roof open. An engine fire wouldn't do that."

"Then we're probably safe," Molly said, letting that last word linger. "Second question: Is anyone else around?"

Javi took a deep breath and called, "Hey! Anybody there?"

Only the birds responded. Molly didn't know much about birds, but these sounded weird. Their squawking slid from pitch to pitch, like a screen door with a rusty hinge.

Suddenly, a *hiss* came from the front of the plane. Something was ballooning into being, a giant arm jutting out!

Oliver screamed, and Molly stepped in front of him. But then she saw the forward emergency exit opening—the giant arm was just another escape slide inflating, flailing madly as it took shape.

"It's okay," she said to Oliver, part of her marveling at how quickly the wadded-up plastic formed into a slide.

Two girls stepped out onto the wing, in identical skirts like school uniforms. They held hands, wobbling a little. A taller boy loomed behind them.

An exhausted shudder of relief went through Molly. If someone else had survived, then maybe Oliver was right, and the rest of the passengers were somewhere out there in this inexplicable jungle.

"Be careful up there!" she shouted, and turned to Oliver and Anna. "You guys help them. We'll keep looking."

Anna started through the undergrowth toward the base of the other slide, signaling for Oliver to follow. He went after her, looking relieved to have something to do.

A moment later, Javi and Molly were alone.

He looked at her with a blank expression. "I hope you don't want any theories or conjectures from me."

Molly swallowed. She didn't know what she wanted, except for things to start making sense. And Javi could help with that. One thing she'd learned from living with her mother: Shared crazy was better than the stuck-in-your-own-head kind.

"Just tell me what you're thinking."

"Okay." Javi's eyes were wide as they swept the surroundings. "This looks like a jungle. But between Tokyo and New York, there's only Canada and Alaska and ocean."

Molly watched as the first of the two girls slid to the ground. "You forgot Hudson Bay."

"Which is still not a jungle," Javi said. "Which means we're way off course. Maybe there was some kind of storm, or a hijacking? And we wound up in . . ." Javi looked up at the trees and shrugged. "South America?"

"We flew thousands of miles due south, and none of us noticed? That doesn't make sense."

"I didn't say it did!" A note of panic crept into Javi's voice.

"Sorry. It's just . . ." Molly shook her head. "Before I fell asleep, there was snow outside my window as far as I could see. And South America would take another twelve hours. What plane carries that much fuel?"

"Sure, right. But where *we* are isn't the big question, is it?" Javi looked up at the silent plane. All those empty windows in a row. "Where are *they*?"

It felt like a sliver of ice was lodged in Molly's throat. "We can't tell Oliver what we're thinking."

"What *are* we thinking?" Javi asked.

Molly hesitated as Anna called up to the second girl. She seemed scared to come down the slide. The taller boy pushed past her and slid first.

Molly cleared her throat. "That lightning that Anna mentioned? I also—"

"Shhh!" Javi cut in. "Did you hear that?"

Molly listened. All she heard was the strange birds and the soft buzz of insects, and a distant rumbling, like a waterfall. But then a sound came from the direction of the plane—a scrabbling.

She turned. In the belly of the aircraft, below the wing, was a long, jagged hole.

"The cargo hold?" Molly whispered.

"It could be a dog or something," Javi said quietly. "Would anyone fly a dog to Japan?"

"Well, we packed soccer-playing robots." Molly headed toward the rent in the airplane's hull, happy to leave the subject of missing passengers behind. "Come on."

The metal was jagged, and the hole was a tight fit. Once they were inside, the cargo hold was pitch-dark. The two of them crept slowly across strewn luggage, moving in silence.

What if something from the jungle had crawled in after the wreck?

Jungles were full of predators. Pythons. Jaguars. Tigers.

Molly reminded herself that none of those things lived in Canada. Grizzly bears, sure, but what would bears be doing in a jungle?

None of this made sense, really. And when logic was a waste of time, fear was probably still useful.

More scrabbling echoed through the darkness.

"Wish we had a flashlight," Javi whispered.

Molly paused. Just in front of her, a shaft of sun shot through a hole in the plane's skin. But the bright spot only made it harder for her eyes to adjust.

Then she saw a piece of metal glittering on the floor.

"Hang on." Molly picked up the metal, then held it in the shaft of sunlight, reflecting a shaky beam into the darkness. She probed the scattered luggage and cargo crates, till she found a figure in the shadows.

"Great," called a voice. "Hold that light steady!"

Molly looked at Javi. Another passenger.

"What are you *doing* down here?" she called.

The figure stood, holding up a hand to shield his eyes in the beam. "Trying to find my luggage! Do you mind not pointing that in my eyes? I'm looking for a sword."

Yoshi

sword?" the voice asked.

Yoshi sighed. "Just look for a long leather case. It's very valuable!"

"Um, okay?" The light wavered, and Yoshi realized that it wasn't a flashlight after all, just something reflecting a shaft of sunlight. And the girl holding it was a kid, maybe a year younger than him.

Where was the crew? And all the other passengers?

Most important, where was his family's seventeenth-century katana?

The light flashed in his eyes again, and Yoshi fought a wave of dizziness . . .

A plane crash. An actual *plane crash*.

Out of everything that could have happened—lost

luggage, snooping customs agents, hijackers—why did it have to be something so random?

He could see his father shaking his head. *Your airplane crashed? Well, you should have thought of that* before *stealing from your homeland.*

The words didn't even make sense, and yet Yoshi could hear them perfectly.

He wondered again if this was all just a nightmare. The plane being torn apart, the weird lights, the impossible jungle outside. And after the crash, crawling down through that smoking rip in the cabin floor, into this jumble of luggage, all of it cheap and ugly and *not his katana.*

"You said a long case, right?" a boy's voice called. "Like, black leather?"

"Yes!" Yoshi pushed his way through the strewn luggage toward where the two figures stood. He saw in silhouette that one of them held something a meter long, about as wide as a paperback book. As Yoshi stumbled nearer, he saw the dangling priority and insurance tags.

"That's it!" He snatched the case from the boy, hefted it, and felt the familiar weight in his hands. Yes, the katana was still inside.

The boy and girl were staring at him, and Yoshi managed to gather himself.

"Thank you," he said, bowing. "I owe you a debt."

"Uh, sure," the boy said. "Glad I could help."

Relief swept through Yoshi. It was all he could do to keep

from opening the case and drawing the sword before their startled eyes, just to make sure it was okay.

"Our friends are outside," the girl said, nodding at a jagged hole in the airplane's skin. "And we found some other people, too."

"Of course," Yoshi said. "Take me to them."

Maybe someone out there knew what was going on.

The sunlight was blinding, the scent of the jungle overwhelming.

It wasn't like anywhere Yoshi had ever seen before—not in textbooks, magazines, or movies. Certainly not in real life. It was more like something from *Jura Tripper*. He half expected to see dinosaurs crashing through the dense undergrowth.

There were five more people outside. The tall white guy with a crew cut was probably the oldest. A white girl, blond and willowy, was about Yoshi's age, and the blond boy and two Japanese girls were younger. The boy and girl who'd found him in the cargo hold both had dark skin and curly hair, but they didn't look like brother and sister. She was wiry and athletic, while he was short and a little out of shape.

A pretty random bunch, except for one thing—nobody was an adult. An odd coincidence, Yoshi thought, but not as weird as everything else that had happened.

They all stared at one another, until the guy with the crew cut began, "I think this is everyone. I've been up and down the plane, and there's nothing but torn-out seats. The ceiling is ripped open the whole way down. It's like the whole plane fell apart in midair!"

The guy was breathing hard, just standing there. He was still amped up from the crash.

Yoshi felt strangely calm inside, like part of him still thought this was all a dream. Or maybe the reassuring weight of the katana was keeping him grounded.

The older boy pointed at a plastic case on the ground at his feet. "I found a survival kit, and I'm sure help is on the way. We just need to get organized. Maybe build a signal fire."

"We can't do that," said the girl who'd been in the cargo hold.

"Sure we can!" The guy knelt and tore open the survival kit. "There's probably a lighter in here somewhere."

"No, I mean . . ." She let out an exasperated sigh. "See that wing with all the dents in it? It's full of jet fuel. If any fumes are leaking, you'll get more than a signal fire. You'll get an explosion they can see on Mars!"

The tall boy looked up at her, still breathing hard, and a tremor passed through the group—a struggle was about to start. But then the boy who'd found Yoshi's katana stepped forward.

"Maybe we should all introduce ourselves," he said. "I'm Javi."

The tension ebbed as the others gave their names. The girl who'd been in the cargo hold was Molly, and their two blond friends were Oliver and Anna. The boy who thought he was in charge was Caleb.

Caleb pointed at the Japanese girls. "They don't speak English." He looked at Yoshi. "Do you?"

Yoshi nodded, then turned to the girls. *"Onamae-wa, nan desu ka?"*

"Kira," said one, bowing.

"Akiko," said the other.

Yoshi raised an eyebrow. Both the names meant *shiny*, and they wore identical skirts. Clearly sisters with easily amused parents, but Kira had dyed a white streak into her hair. Maybe she was the rebel.

"I'm Yoshi Kimura," he finished the introductions.

"Okay." Caleb clapped his hands, as if calling a meeting back to order. "I guess a signal fire isn't necessary. That plane is pretty easy to spot. And it probably has all kinds of black boxes inside, transmitting our location."

Yoshi saw Javi and Molly sharing a look, but Caleb didn't notice.

"Of course, we don't know how long it will take them to get here," he went on. "So we should probably build a shelter."

"A shelter from what?" Molly asked.

Caleb gave her that look again. He wasn't used to being argued with.

Molly kept her eyes straight on his. "It isn't cold enough to need insulation. If it rains, we can camp out under a wing, or one of those inflatable slides. And if a predator comes along, I'd rather be back inside the plane than hiding in some tree fort."

"A predator?" Oliver turned to stare into the jungle.

Anna followed his gaze. "Good point, Molly. That's a pretty big food web out there. There must be something at the top, eating everything else."

Oliver blanched, and Molly glared at Anna.

"There's insects," Javi jumped in again. "I've only been camping one time, but around sundown we got eaten alive."

"Sure," Molly said. "But we can't make insect screens out of palm fronds. This whole idea of building a shelter is silly."

Javi spread his hands. "So maybe we look for bug spray."

Yoshi watched Caleb, whose expression grew more and more astonished. Maybe he was always surprised when people didn't let him run the show.

But no one was asking the real questions.

Why had a plane flying over the Arctic landed in a jungle? And where were all the other passengers? Was everyone else *dead*?

Yoshi shook off the thought. It was pointless guessing at something so awful before taking a look around.

"Bug spray?" A note of anger rose in Caleb's voice, or maybe it was panic. "Don't you realize how serious this is?"

"Why are you all arguing?" Oliver cried. "None of this makes sense, and everyone's gone! And *where's Mr. Keating*?"

His words descended into sobs, and silence fell on the group. Molly looked stricken, like she was about to cry, too—or punch someone. Kira and Akiko stood closer together, their hands finding each other's.

Yoshi closed his eyes for a moment. His father had always said that manga and anime were distractions, that he should

- 38 -

focus on reality instead. But now that reality was right here, staring him in the face, Yoshi knew exactly what to do.

He knelt by the open survival kit. It took a few seconds to find a canteen, a compass, and a two-way radio. Then he clicked open the hasps on his case, checked the oil and powder, the cleaning cloth—all there—and pulled out the katana. Lifting the strap over his head, he felt the elegant curve of the scabbard settle between his shoulder blades. As the others watched in silence, Yoshi pocketed the oil and cleaning cloth and snapped the case closed.

"I'll be back before dark," he said.

Caleb stood tall. "Uh, *Yoshi*, right? Where do you think you're going?"

"To find water. I'll leave the tree fort and bug spray to you guys."

There was a moment of silence as the others registered his words. Water wasn't about comfort—it was about survival.

"There were water bottles on the plane," Javi said.

Yoshi nodded. "We'll need all of them. But we won't last very long unless we can refill them. You all realize that, right?"

When no one answered, Yoshi sighed and held out his arms, indicating the trees, the jungle, the white sky.

"Something very strange happened. We're in the wrong place. Not Canada or Alaska. Not Japan. We have no idea when rescue is coming. Water is the first step to surviving this."

Oliver made a small, frightened noise, and Molly moved to take his hand. The others just stared at Yoshi, and for the first time Caleb seemed to have nothing to say.

Yoshi held up the radio. "I have this, so once you find another survival kit, we'll be able to communicate." He turned to the two girls and switched to Japanese. "I'll be back soon. It'll be okay."

Akiko nodded nervously. "Be careful, Yoshi. There might be something bad out there."

He smiled and lifted his right hand behind his head to take the hilt of the katana. He drew it just a little, exposing a few inches of bright, razor-sharp metal.

"I'll be fine."

Anna

"Flashlight, batteries, food bars, knife, radio, matches, and fire starters. Whistle, flares, signal mirror, water purification pills, canteen, compass, and first-aid kit. It's all here."

Anna put the list back inside the survival kit and sat back. Putting everything they had scavenged from the plane into piles made her feel better, somehow. As if every problem had a solution.

As if the world still made sense, and Mr. Keating and five hundred other people hadn't just disappeared.

The two sisters sat before her. Kira—the one with the bleached white streak in her hair—was sketching everything. Her pencil made little skittering sounds above the buzz of insects. Akiko still seemed stunned from the crash, and when

Kira murmured to her in Japanese—or sometimes what sounded like French—she didn't answer.

Anna picked up the survival knife. One side of its blade was serrated, like a saw. Or was that for cleaning fish?

"Knife," she said.

Kira didn't look up. She was busy drawing the Aero Horizon logo from the survival kit's cover. But Akiko looked up timidly.

"*Naifu*," she repeated.

"Mirror," Anna said, pointing at the signal mirror.

"*Mira*," Akiko said.

Anna nodded, remembering to smile. But the mirror was probably worthless. A passing plane would never spot the flash of a three-inch reflector through the dense white cloud overhead. The sky seemed endless and formless, impenetrable.

On top of which, she hadn't heard any engine noises since the crash. Even stranger, the compasses didn't work—their needles just spun in lazy circles. Anna found herself wondering if they'd landed on an entirely different planet.

She'd heard of alien abductions of people, but never of a whole airplane.

Of course, there were those airplanes that just vanished . . .

She shook off the thought, which made the numbness descend on her again.

Which tools were the most important for the two Japanese girls to learn the names of? There were so many, all representing different ways to die—dehydration, disease, injury, starvation.

She pointed. "Food bar."

"Fudoba," Akiko said.

"Close enough," Anna said with a shrug. If they were stuck here long enough for the girls to learn fluent English, they were all in deep trouble.

Akiko picked up the radio.

"Radio," Anna said carefully.

Akiko repeated the word, then turned on the radio and said Yoshi's name into it. For a moment, they all listened for a response.

Nothing but the hiss of static.

"He's probably not dead," Anna said to herself. "Just too far away."

"Nineteen more!" Javi called from the wing, his arms full of water bottles. He jumped onto the escape slide and zipped down.

As he added the bottles to the water pile, Anna did the math aloud.

"That's eighty-one. Ten bottles per person, plus one. Enough for two days, maybe three."

"That's not very long," Javi said.

"It isn't," Anna said. "There's a rule about how people die. Two minutes without oxygen. Two days without water. Two weeks without food."

"Um, you're doing that thing," Javi said.

Anna frowned. Molly and Javi always said she was too blunt, especially when talking to people who weren't engineers.

"But it's just you," she said. "The girls don't speak English."

"Yeah, but I'm freaking out, too!" A shudder went through Javi. "We just were in a *plane crash*."

"I know that," Anna said.

"Yeah, well, that's on the list of things that make me *not* an engineer. Right now I'm just a freaked-out regular person!"

"Okay. But it seems like having only five days before we die of dehydration is important information."

"True." Javi sighed. "But we're not going to die. We'll get rescued, or it'll rain, or Yoshi will find water out there. *Something* has to go right eventually."

His voice cracked a little at the end, so Anna nodded reassuringly.

Yoshi had the right idea, looking for a source of water. Maybe he'd been a little too dramatic with his exit, not taking a flashlight, food, or any water—just an empty canteen.

But at least Yoshi wasn't afraid to *do* something.

And he'd certainly looked impressive with that sword on his back.

She hoped he was okay.

"Can I see the knife?" Javi asked.

Anna handed it over. "Don't lose it. There's only one per kit."

They'd found three survival packs in the plane. According to the crew manual that Oliver had discovered, a fourth kit had been in the missing tail section. Which had to be somewhere nearby . . .

Or did this jungle simply swallow things?

Anna remembered the passengers being lifted out of the crashing plane. Mr. Keating sitting right next to her, then gone.

She squashed the thought down. *Focus on what's in front of you.*

"That's one for each of us in Team Killbot." Javi made a swiping motion. "I don't trust Caleb with a knife, and Yoshi's got that baller ninja sword."

Anna looked out into the jungle. It was growing darker, the insects louder. Yoshi's sword wouldn't protect him from getting lost.

"Find any more food?" she asked.

"Just nuts and fruit, and some cheese. The meals were still frozen, and this heat is turning them into airplane food slush."

"Gross," Anna said. "Also, food poisoning."

"Almost barfed." Javi looked up at the plane. "Are Molly and Oliver still in the front?"

"No, they finished. They're in the luggage hold now." Anna frowned. "Oliver keeps saying he shouldn't be here."

"Oh, crud." Javi swallowed. "You know his mother wasn't going to let him come to Japan. Molly talked her into it."

Anna nodded. "But Oliver talked Molly into talking his mother into it. He *wanted* to come."

"Yeah," Javi sighed. "But maybe he's changed his mind for some inexplicable reason. Did they find anything useful in the plane? Like, three hundred miles of wire?"

Anna pointed at the pile: backpacks, blankets, plastic bags, soap and shampoo from someone's carry-on, and a handful of phones—no signal, but maybe they'd be useful as flashlights. Also two of the Killbots, which Molly had salvaged first from the cargo hold.

"Soccer-playing robots. Super useful," Javi said. He started to hand the knife back to Anna, but Kira reached up and plucked it from his hand.

"*Naifu*," she said solemnly, then placed it on the ground and began to draw it. Her Aero Horizon logo was finished—a nearly perfect copy, Anna noticed.

Javi pointed at the trees. "So do your biology thing. Is there any food we can eat out there?"

"Of course," Anna said. "The problem is, *we're* food out there."

He glanced at Kira and the knife. "We can protect ourselves."

Anna shook her head. "Nature's full of stuff that isn't afraid of knives. Like poisonous plants, bloodsucking insects, parasites that eat you from the inside."

Javi gave a dramatic sigh. "You're always so comforting, Anna. And just so you know, I'm being *super* sarcastic."

Anna had known, and sometimes Javi's sarcasm was funny, but not now. She still felt that numbness that had overtaken her after the crash. Too many things didn't seem real about this. The missing passengers. The weird jungle. Even the darting birds sounded wrong.

Of course, the birds were probably edible. But how to catch one?

A *clunk* came from the pile next to the water bottles. Akiko was rummaging through it, taking a closer look at everything.

"What's all that junk?" Javi asked.

Anna shrugged. "Stuff that the girls found in the wreckage behind the plane."

Akiko held up something questioningly. Black plastic straps woven together.

Anna frowned. It looked like something designed to keep luggage from bouncing around in the hold. "Cargo webbing?"

Akiko repeated the words haltingly, then picked up another piece of wreckage.

Anna took it from her, peering closer. "Huh. I don't know."

The device was donut-shaped, a little too big and heavy to be a bracelet. A set of symbols went around the outside of the ring, another on the inside. Anna didn't recognize any of them.

Was it aircraft equipment of some kind? An antenna? A transmitter?

Now *that* would be useful.

Anna looked for a switch to turn it on. Nothing.

"Probably just a toy," Javi said. He was bouncing on the bottom section of the inflatable slide, making the plastic squeak.

"Probably." Anna looked up at his bouncing. "You know if you puncture that slide, Molly will kill you, right?"

"I'm testing its strength," Javi said, still bouncing. "And it's not like we need a life raft."

"We could collect rainwater with it." Anna turned back to the unknown device. There was a groove along the inside. If she could twist it open and see its guts, maybe she could figure out what it was.

But when Anna twisted, the device didn't open—its outer symbols slid clockwise, each aligning with one of the inner symbols.

"Hmm," she said. "Looks like some kid's secret decoder ring."

Javi laughed. "An essential part of every jungle survival kit!"

"Yeah. Unless it has some kind of batteries we can . . ." Her voice faded. Two of the aligned symbols—one outer, one inner—lit up, pulsing for a moment.

"That's funny," she said.

"Funny ha-ha or funny strange?" Javi asked, still bouncing.

She pressed the symbols, and they stayed lit. The device began to tremble in her hands. "Funny . . . scary?"

"That's not a funny."

"It is now," Anna said. Her head went light and fuzzy, and then she realized something really weird.

The object wasn't heavy anymore.

A moment ago, it had felt like metal in her hand. But now it weighed no more than hollow plastic.

"Um, this is odd," Javi said.

She looked up at him. "What is?"

Javi opened his mouth to speak, but nothing came out. His expression turned to queasy astonishment as he descended— *way* too slowly—back down onto the inflatable slide.

His next bounce carried him high into the air.

9

Javi

"What the . . ." Javi started.

He was still climbing, wafting up toward the white sky. But he had no sense of motion or momentum. It didn't feel like flying, exactly, more like the ground was falling away. It was as if the crashed plane and the jungle itself had all been fake, a film set that was dropping away beneath him, leaving him here, suspended in midair.

He stared down at Anna and the two girls, who stared back up at him. The device still flickered in Anna's hand. The air seemed to ripple around her.

The machine was doing this—whatever *this* was. Javi's guts felt suspended in his body. His clothes didn't hang on him. Everything floated together, weightless.

Was he ever going to stop climbing? Or would he just go up forever until he disappeared into the white cloud above?

No. Javi realized that he was slowing at last, then falling toward earth again. Though it felt more like the other way around—the ground was rising up to meet him, as slow and stately as a giant ship easing into port.

Down below, Kira was floating, too, only a few feet in the air. Her sketch pad and the survival knife hovered beside her, and the bottom of the inflatable slide was wafting up.

Anna's long hair was floating wildly around her head. It was like gravity had been canceled. Or at least dialed way down.

Which meant that when he hit the slide again, Javi would bounce up again. Not good.

As he drifted downward, Javi readied himself to crumple his legs. Like on a trampoline, he would stifle all that energy with his own body.

But the moment before he hit the inflated plastic, a completely different idea—a wild, irrational one—overtook him.

Maybe he should go *higher*.

His first bounce had taken him almost to the tops of the trees pressed in tight around the airplane. They hid the rest of the jungle, and anything else that might be out there. But now Javi had a chance to see beyond them, from a bird's-eye view.

More than anything else, he wanted to know *what on earth was going on*.

So when his feet touched down, he bent his knees, then launched himself upward as hard as he could. Straight into the sky.

"What are you doing?" cried Anna.

"Taking a look!"

Javi shot higher, until he was above the trees, staring down at the broken plane laid out across the jungle. He saw how its spine gaped open as if a giant claw had traveled down it, how the wing on the far side lay snapped in two.

He gazed back along the trail of the landing path. The first marks of the crash were miles away, where the plane's belly had sheared off the jungle canopy. A little closer were the trees bent by its passage, and finally the splintered remains of those it had ripped straight through.

The jungle was so *thick*. Cutting through a mile of that dense growth, the plane should have been torn to pieces. Just like it should have tumbled out of control from the sky, instead of coming down in a straight line.

But something had protected it.

Javi looked around—nothing but jungle in all directions, though the mist made it hard to see very far.

He heard a rumbling, though. He'd felt it down on the ground, a low, persistent noise that seemed to come from everywhere. But from this height Javi could hear where it actually came from—in the distance off to the left of the crashed plane.

It sounded like a waterfall. Which meant there had to be water around somewhere.

As he began to descend again, Javi felt a sudden jolt of panic. If gravity came back now, the bouncy slide wouldn't be enough to save him. His legs would break, and his guts would turn to jelly.

Why had he jumped so high?

"Don't panic," he told himself, and surveyed the jungle one last time, to make this trip into the sky worthwhile.

Way out there, he saw something beyond the trees. At the horizon, in the direction the plane was pointed, something flat and formless glimmered.

But a moment later Javi was too low to see anything but trees . . . and birds.

Screeching like demons, a flock was skimming through the jungle canopy. They were small, bright green, and formed into a tight pack. They seemed to ripple among the branches, the sunlight glinting from their long, sharp beaks.

They were coming right at Javi.

Maybe he should try to scare them off?

"Shoo!" he shouted, waving his arms as he slowly fell.

But the birds kept coming, and he barely had time to cover his face before the whole flock shot past in a roar of feathers and shrieks.

"Ahhh!" he yelled, feeling slivers of pain open up all over him, like a dozen paper cuts had appeared on his skin. Why were *birds* attacking him?

Javi opened his eyes after the fluttering had passed. His shirt was ripped and torn, and blood seeped through in a few places. The backs of his hand were bleeding, too—he'd covered his face just in time.

He was still falling toward the ground, but not fast enough. The flock was whirling around again, coming at him.

"Help!" he yelled.

Anna was looking up in horror. She grabbed one of the floating pieces of metal from the wreckage pile—the emergency door. It had weighed maybe sixty pounds, back before gravity was optional. But Anna sent it hurtling toward him like it was a cafeteria tray.

What was he supposed to do with it, though? Use it as a shield?

The birds were closing in when Anna shouted, "Third law of motion!"

Javi tried to think. Every action has an equal and opposite reaction? Like jumping forward from a skateboard, and it rolls backward . . .

Just in time, he understood. He grabbed the emergency door as it passed, which sent him spinning, then hurled it as hard as he could straight up into the air.

Which sent him careening straight down toward the ground.

The flock of birds shot past again but most of them missed, passing overhead. One bird crashed satisfyingly into the door, and a floating cloud of feathers exploded above Javi.

The flock was already wheeling around again. But he was descending much faster now, thanks to the door.

Below him, Kira had stuck the survival knife into the ground. She was clinging to it with one hand, and to Akiko with the other.

As Javi hit the slide, he imagined himself bouncing back up into the air and being torn to pieces. But then Anna did something with the device . . .

Full-strength gravity hit like a punch in the gut, and Javi flopped back onto the inflated plastic. There was a clatter as the floating piles of water bottles, survival tools, and wreckage all hit the ground together, along with grunts from Kira and Akiko.

"Incoming!" Anna cried out. "Get under the slide!"

Kira and Akiko were already crawling under cover. Javi tried to scramble off the plastic, but his muscles felt weird and wobbly. He slipped to the ground just as the roar of the flock filled the air above him . . .

. . . and kept going.

He looked up and saw the birds disappearing into the trees.

"Javi!" Anna screamed. "Get under here!"

He shook his head. "They just—"

"Door!" she cried, as a huge metal *crunk* came from behind Javi, making him leap into the air.

He spun around to find the emergency door crumpled on the ground. It had gouged a fat hole in the dirt, maybe five feet from where he stood.

"Whoa," Anna said as she emerged, staring at the door. "I forgot about that when I turned the gravity back on. Are you okay?"

Javi looked down at himself. He was covered with tiny cuts, but none of the razor-sharp beaks had found a vein. Just lucky, he supposed. And he'd been lucky with the falling emergency door, too.

But the prospect of being crushed wasn't why his knees were shaking. What was making Javi feel sick was the phrase that Anna had just uttered so casually.

When I turned the gravity back on.

What *was* that thing?

Molly

We have to go look for Yoshi," Molly said. "It's not safe out there."

Caleb crossed his arms. "Not a good idea."

"Look at what those birds did!" She pointed at Javi. His shirt hung in ribbons, and the bandages from a first-aid kit were strewn across his torso. "Yoshi doesn't know about them, and he's been gone for hours. That means he's miles away, and lost!"

"It's too dangerous out there," Caleb said. "We could get lost, too!"

"We'll figure something out." Molly's mind raced. The compasses didn't work, and the clouds were too thick to navigate by the sun. They couldn't even tell how soon night would fall, but she didn't dare mention that to Caleb. "Maybe we can mark our path, like with bread crumbs."

"Bread crumbs?" Oliver murmured. "I'd rather eat them."

Molly looked at him. "Sorry—*metaphorical* bread crumbs. Or we could build something taller than the trees. Something we can see from far away."

The two inflatable slides stacked up would have been perfect. But one of them was growing more limp by the minute, hanging from the wing like an old rag doll. It had been torn when all the wreckage had come tumbling down.

Everything was going wrong.

Including *gravity*.

Molly and Oliver had heard the shouting and had come out the front emergency exit just in time to see it all. Javi suspended in midair, attacked by the flock of screeching birds. Kira and Akiko floating a few feet off the ground, along with the water bottles, survival gear, and everything else that wasn't nailed down. And Anna with that *thing* in her hands, the air pulsing and rippling around her.

Anna still held the device, clinging to it like it was a winning lottery ticket. Kira stood next to her, drawing the symbols one by one.

"I'm not sure what you kids got up to while I was gone." Caleb spread his hands to encompass the strewn survival gear, Javi's wounds, the sagging slide. "But you made a mess."

"What we *got up to* was changing how gravity worked!" Javi cried. "And you're worried about a mess?"

Caleb gave Javi the same sarcastic look as when he'd first heard the story. "Right. You found a toy that let you fly."

"Not fly, jump," Javi said. "It turns down gravity, somehow."

"But now it doesn't work anymore," Caleb said with a snort. "That's convenient."

Anna shrugged, handing the device over. Caleb stared at the symbols, gave a tired sigh, then tossed it back. He didn't notice how Akiko and Kira flinched when he touched it.

Molly had to agree that the machine's sudden failure was a little *too* convenient. She wondered what Anna was up to.

"Whatever happened here," Caleb said, "I'm not going to let you go marching off into the jungle."

Molly laughed. "*Let* us go into the jungle?"

Caleb stood taller, his muscles bulging. "You heard what I said."

"Who died and made you scoutmaster?" Molly asked.

He looked at her, totally serious. "About five hundred people."

The words hit like a punch in the stomach, and without thinking Molly turned to Oliver and put an arm around him.

Till now, no one had said it out loud—no one else on the plane had survived. Mr. Keating, the crew, all those other passengers—rows and rows of people had filed into the aircraft's countless seats, and now they were all gone. Flung out into the jungle somewhere back there.

No one spoke. Kira had even stopped drawing, sensing that something serious was being discussed.

"It's true, isn't it?" Oliver said. "They're all dead."

Molly squeezed him. "We don't really know what happened, Oliver. None of this makes sense."

He pulled away, fists clenched. "Anna said she *saw* them being thrown out."

Molly glared at Anna, hoping she wouldn't mention the weird lightning they'd seen on the plane. If Oliver lost it now, the rest of Team Killbot might just fall apart.

But it was Javi who spoke up first. "The important thing right now is to find Yoshi."

"You're right," Molly said thankfully. "Figuring out what happened can wait."

Oliver looked like he wanted to say more, but he just shook his head and looked away. There was a moment of tense silence.

Luckily, Caleb still wanted to argue. "We're not going to find anyone in that jungle. It's pointless to try."

"Okay, scoutmaster," Molly said. "Then what's *your* plan to help Yoshi?"

"Maybe if we made a sound." Caleb gave a shrug. "Something he could hear from miles away. So he can find his own way back."

Molly frowned—it wasn't a *terrible* idea. "But if he's close enough to hear us, wouldn't his radio work?"

"It could be broken."

"The plane was full of alarms," Javi said. "They went off while it was crashing. We just need power to run them."

Oliver wiped his nose with the back of his shirtsleeve. "We've got plenty of flashlight batteries."

"We'll work on that," Anna said. "And we won't make a mess, Caleb, we promise. But maybe you can scout around in the meantime? Just in case Yoshi's somewhere nearby, and he's hurt."

Caleb gave them all a long look, like he still thought they were up to no good. But finally he nodded, grabbed a knife and a flashlight from the open survival kit, and headed off into the underbrush.

Kira went back to drawing, and Akiko picked up a flute she'd found in the wreckage. She began to play a soft, mournful tune.

Molly looked at Javi and Anna and Oliver.

"Okay, team. What's the real plan?"

Javi glanced in the direction Caleb had gone. "When I was up in the air, I could hear a waterfall. Off to the left of the plane."

"Yoshi was looking for water," Anna said. "If he hears it, he'll go that way sooner or later."

Molly shook her head. "But he must be miles away by now. And Caleb's right—if his radio doesn't work, we'll never find him. You can't see more than a few feet in that jungle!"

"Not from the ground." Anna held up the device. "But from up in the treetops?"

Molly stared at her. "So *why* exactly did you tell Caleb it was broken?"

"Yeah," Javi said. "Way to make me look like a liar."

"But in certain situations, lying is okay. Like not telling people when their haircut looks bad, or preventing dangerous technology from falling into the wrong hands." Anna hefted the device. "There's no way Caleb understands how amazing this is. I mean, gravity is a law of nature, a fundamental force, and this thing turns it off like a light switch."

"So?" Molly asked. "If you'd just show him how it works, he'd have to believe you."

"But he thinks he's in charge. What's to stop him from taking it?"

Molly took a slow breath. Caleb was bigger than the rest of them and willing to use force, she had a feeling. Maybe handing over an incredible, and possibly dangerous, machine wasn't such a great idea.

"What does it feel like?" Oliver asked. "When there's no gravity?"

"Stand very still," Anna said, and twisted the outside of the device while pushing down on two of the weird symbols scattered around its edge. The symbols glowed, and a heat-ripple traveled through the air. Molly felt her insides shifting a little, like she was in an elevator headed downward, fast.

"Whoa," she said quietly. Javi was grinning, the girls held hands, and Oliver looked like he was about to puke.

Then everything got much weirder—a gust of breeze passed through the jungle, and all six of them lifted a little into the air and wafted sideways, carried along like scraps of paper in the wind.

Anna twisted the device again, and they dropped back to earth, suddenly heavy and stumbling.

"Okay," Molly said as her body settled to earth. "Just *wow*. I felt like I weighed nothing."

"*Almost* nothing." Anna pointed at the crumpled emergency door. "After I turned gravity back on, that took about six seconds to fall. Do the math, Oliver."

Oliver's eyes rolled up in his head. "Falling stuff accelerates at thirty-two feet per second squared—in normal gravity, I mean. And six times thirty-two is about two hundred. So it was going two hundred feet a second when it hit, which means it averaged a hundred feet per second if it started from a standstill. Which means you threw it . . . six hundred feet into the air?"

Even Anna looked surprised at that. For a moment, no one made a sound.

Molly had seen the door hit. Heard it, too—the *crunch* of aircraft metal moving fast enough to squish a human like a bug. A little reminder that everything about this situation was seriously dangerous.

"So who made that thing?" Javi finally said. "And why was it on our plane?"

"And is *that* what made us crash?" Oliver added. "Airplanes are designed to fly in normal gravity. Weird physics would totally mess up the airflow."

Molly's mind was spinning again. At last they had a concrete clue about what was going on, but a device that changed the laws of physics was too much to process. "Maybe there was more than one of those in the cargo hold. Maybe one of them malfunctioned."

"But that doesn't explain the top ripping open," Anna said. "That wasn't weird gravity. It looked intentional."

"You mean *evil*," Oliver said softly.

Molly swallowed. *Evil* was a pretty scary word to use, but it sure seemed like *something* had taken control of the plane, and it hadn't cared who got killed in the process.

"It still could've been the machine." Javi pointed at Kira's drawing of the symbols. "When you turned that thing on, only two of those symbols glowed. What do all the *other* ones do?"

They all stared at the device.

Anna's fingers lightly touched the symbols. "I guess we could find out."

"No way!" Oliver said, taking a step back.

"It's okay." Molly put a hand on Anna's shoulder. "Now's not the time for experimenting. Finding Yoshi is more important."

"I guess," Anna said with a sigh. "But we can use it to fly, right? We head toward the water?"

"Exactly," Molly said. "You stay here, Oliver, and look after the girls. And get started on those alarms, in case we get lost. Maybe Yoshi will hear them and make it back on his own."

"Sure," Oliver said, still eyeing the gravity device warily. "Just watch out for those birds."

Javi tugged at one of the tears in his shirt. "Don't worry, we will."

Molly nodded, remembering the shrieks cutting through the air. "We should bring flares, in case they're afraid of fire. Any other questions?"

"Just one," Oliver said, pointing at the device. "Who *made* that thing?"

They all stared at Molly, as if expecting her to say something.

She could only shrug. She had a feeling that whatever the answer was, they weren't going to find it anytime soon.

11

Yoshi

The water made no sense.

Yoshi frowned. The pool felt as cold as the natural springs the last time he'd gone camping. But that had been in the mountains of Hokkaido, where the water came from melting snows. This place was a rain forest, the air so hot that Yoshi had stripped off his shirt hours ago, tying it around his waist.

He looked up. The waterfall tumbled down from some-place high in the mists, striking the stone outcrop in front of him and splitting into a hundred sprays.

Why was it so cold? Where did it come from?

Of course, the more important question was whether it was drinkable.

Swift-running water meant fewer microbes, he remembered

from his father's survival lectures. And ice-cold was probably better as well.

But the best argument for drinking it was that Yoshi was very, very thirsty. Besides, if the water here was unsafe, he and the other survivors were all doomed anyway.

Yoshi knelt and cupped a handful.

The cold made his teeth hurt, and the taste of minerals and vegetation filled his mouth. But every sip was a relief for his parched lips. He'd set off on this expedition with an empty canteen.

He didn't need his father's voice in his head to tell him that had been foolish.

Yoshi drank his thirst away, then filled the canteen. He turned on the radio again.

"Hello? Molly? Anyone?"

He waited. Nothing but static.

Yoshi sighed and took out the compass. Just like it had all afternoon, the needle spun in lazy circles. And he hadn't been able to navigate by the sun, thanks to the ever-present white cloud overhead.

It was like this place was *designed* to make exploration impossible.

But as Yoshi took a slow drink from the canteen, a sound caught his ears. He frowned and picked up the radio again, holding it closer. Through the static came a soft burbling sound, beeps and tones that he could just hear over the roar of the waterfall.

Like a coded transmission.

Then he saw the compass in his hand—the needle was quivering, pointing straight at the waterfall.

He looked into the mist overhead, wondering again what was up there.

But a moment later, the beeping faded back into static, and the compass needle went back to slowly spinning.

He pressed the transmit button on the radio. "Hello?"

Yoshi listened. Nothing but static.

He pressed the button again. "Is anyone out there?"

Still nothing.

Yoshi sighed. Maybe he had imagined it all. His head was fuzzy from jet lag and no sleep. A cold swim might help.

No point in taking off his clothes. They needed washing, too.

Yoshi made his way to a dry rock that loomed over the deepest part of the pool. He took off his shoes and katana and laid them on the rock.

It took a long time, gathering his nerve to jump. Worse than the freezing water was the thought of leaving his sword out of reach.

For the last mile or so, Yoshi had heard a soft rustling underfoot. Like something was shadowing him, slithering low to the ground, at the edge of hearing.

Of course, it was probably just small animals moving through the undergrowth. Rodents or snakes, or those weirdly large insects he'd seen clinging to the tree trunks—bright green praying mantises with heads the size of pinecones.

Whatever was making the sound, it probably wasn't interested in Yoshi. And now that the roar of the waterfall had swallowed the jungle's sounds, the memory seemed like something else he'd imagined.

Yoshi reached one bare toe down into the water.

Bad idea. A shiver went deep into his bones, sapping his will.

Behind the roar of the waterfall, he sensed a larger sound. Something vast and sovereign, like the rumble of the sea.

He was just stalling, Yoshi knew. He heard his father's voice.

Leap in, or admit you aren't up to it. Don't dither like a coward.

That was motivation enough—Yoshi jumped.

The freezing water enveloped him like a crushing fist. His muscles flinched all at once, squeezing the breath from his lungs. Here underwater, the roar of the fall was a thousand times louder, crowding every thought from his head. Shudders surged through him, and when his feet brushed the muddy bottom, Yoshi kicked himself upward as hard as he could.

He rose above the surface, sputtering for air, and swam straight toward the edge of the pool. He crawled out and lay there, panting and shivering on a mat of vines.

It took a while to recover from the grip of the cold. But finally he sat up, pulled his sopping shirt from around his waist, and laid it out flat.

Yoshi grinned at himself. He'd found water, and after hours of marching through the jungle and sweating, he felt clean at last.

But then the slithering sound came again.

It was barely there under the roar of the waterfall. But Yoshi had seen something, too—a movement among the vines.

His whole body tensed.

Was it a snake? Something poisonous?

He glanced up at the rock where his katana lay. Maybe three steps away.

But no sword could move faster than a snake's strike. The best thing was to sit here, absolutely motionless.

Another rustle among the vines. Closer.

Even with his skin chilled from the water, Yoshi felt a trickle of sweat course down his back.

Suddenly, the rustling was everywhere, like an army of rats had emerged from holes in the ground. Yoshi stared, but couldn't see anything through the red-tinged vines.

What was moving down there?

His heart beat faster, and he glanced again at his sword. The rock was bare, with no vines to hide scurrying creatures.

Should he just jump back into the water?

The thought of that icy cold enveloping him again made him shudder—and at that moment the trembling of the vines stopped.

Yoshi felt a tautness in the air. Like something was waiting for him to make the first move.

He couldn't just *sit* here. His father's voice came again . . .

Don't dither like a coward.

Sudden determination flowed through his muscles, and Yoshi leaped up. His bare feet sank into the vines as he ran for the rock.

But as he jumped for the katana, he felt himself trip. His weight pitched forward, and he fell face-first toward hard stone. His hands came out and broke the fall, the skin of his palms scraping, his wrists screaming with pain.

He tried to free his feet, but something held his ankle. It was trying to drag him back away from his sword . . .

Yoshi reached for the katana, his fingers barely closing around the hilt. He waved it once to fling the scabbard away—the steel blade flashed.

He spun to face his attacker.

12

Anna

Flying was the bomb.

The jungle slipped beneath Anna, brimming with the shrieks of birds, the buzz of insects. Three-fourths of Team Killbot skimmed the canopy like a hot-air balloon, the treetops brushing their feet.

It wasn't technically *flying*, Anna reminded herself. She, Javi, and Molly couldn't maintain their altitude. They wafted down every thirty seconds or so, crashing softly into the web of branches before pushing off again.

But even if it was only jumping—it was jumping *really* far. Each push took them hundreds of feet through the mists.

Molly had found bungee cords in someone's luggage, and the team was tied together so nobody drifted out of the gravity device's range, which was about thirty feet. The three of them had learned to jump in tandem to keep from spinning like a bola, but whenever a gust of wind stirred the misty treetops, it carried them adrift.

Anna wondered if there was a way to control their flight. Maybe if they made wings? Or some kind of fan, like the propellers on an airship?

"Yoshi! Are you out there?" Molly cried out at the top of their next leap.

Anna listened as they arced downward into the treetops. No answer, except for a stirring of the birds that sounded like rusty hinges.

She had distinguished four species by sound: the rusty-hinge birds, the cranky-baby birds, the slide-whistle birds, and of course the shredder birds. Luckily, she hadn't heard any of those since they'd attacked Javi back at camp.

"Okay," Molly called. "Looks like this tree's yours, Javi."

"I got it."

Their next landing tree was coming right at Javi, who was in the middle of the three of them. As they descended into the canopy, he reached out and grabbed the passing treetop. Anna felt the bungee cord pull at her waist, then she swung in a slow arc past Molly coming from the other direction. Their combined momentum bent the tree, like a catapult readying to fire. It swung back, trying to throw them in the direction they'd just come from.

Javi clung on grimly as the treetop swayed back and forth to a gradual stop.

"I still don't love flying."

"Are you kidding?" Molly laughed at him. "This is awesome!"

"I concur," Anna said. Even with the laws of physics bending around them, this was the most normal she'd felt since the crash. The numbness inside her was finally lifting. Maybe it was the jungle stretched out below her, full of life and color and sound. Or maybe it was getting away from the crashed plane and its gaping rows of torn-out seats.

"There's something I don't get," Javi said as the three untangled their bungee cords. "If we barely weigh anything, how come we bend the treetops so much?"

"Yeah, and my legs are getting sore," Molly said. "Even with gravity switched off, this is hard work."

Anna's mind spun a moment, and the answer came. "We're like an asteroid. Rocks in space are totally weightless, but they can still crush you. They have momentum, they have—"

"Mass!" Javi cried out.

"Right," Anna said. "Remember when Mr. Keating explained the difference between weight and mass?"

Molly looked away, and Anna realized what she had said. In her mind's eye she saw Mr. Keating being lifted into the air and flung from the plane. The numbness closed in again, like she was packed in mud.

An awkward silence fell over the group.

"Sorry," Anna finally said.

"It's okay," Molly said. "But maybe don't mention him in front of Oliver."

"I don't want to talk about it, either," Anna said. "I just want to jump. And find Yoshi. I like him."

Molly smiled. "Me too. You guys ready?"

Anna checked the bungee cord connecting her to Javi and nodded. They pushed off, hard, and soon Team Killbot was arcing through the air again, leaving dark thoughts behind.

As they drifted up into the mists, Molly cried out, "You out there, Yoshi?"

Anna listened but heard nothing except the calls of slide-whistle birds. She tried the radio again, which only sputtered with the usual static.

"Check that out," Javi called, pointing.

Thrusting up from the surface of the jungle canopy was a stand of much taller trees. They were spindly and thin-trunked, crisscrossed with vines. They reached so high that their tops were lost in the mist.

And they seemed to be arranged in a perfect circle.

"That's weird," Anna said.

"Yeah," Molly said. "It looks like someone *planted* them that way."

Anna looked at her. "Mind if we take a detour?"

Molly nodded, and on the next jump, they angled their path toward the taller trees.

As they drew nearer, Anna saw that the area was buzzing with life. Bright flowers covered the trees, and iridescent lizards leaped from vine to vine. A cacophony of birds filled the branches, shrieking as they jostled with each other.

It was almost deafening but, just barely, Anna could hear another noise from deep within the stand of trees.

A very familiar noise.

It sounded like a half-clogged drainpipe sputtering up blood and gristle, like a wild boar trying to form words in some hideous unknown language. It sent a ten-foot icicle up Anna's spine.

Shredder birds. Lots of them.

"Uh-oh," Anna said.

"Plan A!" Molly called. She reached into her jacket pocket and pulled out a signal flare.

With a horrible gabble, a ripple of green emerged from the taller trees, at least a hundred birds in tight formation. Molly tore off the top of the flare. It sputtered to life, sparks and smoke trailing behind her as she flew.

The flock of shredder birds reacted, coiling away from the hissing flame . . .

And heading straight toward Anna.

Anna realized the problem with Plan A—with the three of them spread out on bungee cords, she was too far from the flame.

She went for her own flare.

"Save it!" Molly yelled. "Javi, pull us closer together!"

Javi grabbed both the cords leading from his belt and yanked. Anna felt herself slewing sideways through the air, headed in toward Javi. Molly came flying in from the opposite side, the flare hissing in her hand.

The birds' formation split and went shrieking in all directions, a storm of wings enveloping Team Killbot just as Anna and Molly crashed into each other. Anna clung to the gravity device and Molly shrieked—the smell of burning hair filling Anna's lungs. The two bounced back, tumbling through the air, and Anna saw the flare go spinning down into the jungle.

"Ouch! Crap!" Molly yelled, batting at her smoking hair.

Anna looked at the shredder birds. They had streamed past, but a moment later the flock was wheeling around again.

"Incoming," she said.

"I'll use mine!" Javi held his flare up.

"No! We've only got two more!" Molly cried. "Go to Plan B."

Anna smiled—she'd been really wanting to try Plan B.

She switched the device off, then back on again as quickly as she could. A sickening jolt of normal gravity hit her stomach.

Weightlessness came back a moment later, but the sudden burst of gravity had bent their course, sending the three of them downward through the trees. The shrieking birds missed again, passing overhead as fronds and branches slapped at Anna's face. Then a bungee cord snagged and went taut. Anna found herself spinning, wrapping around a tree like a tetherball.

Finally, she crashed into Javi, sending a shower of leaves in all directions.

"Ow," he said.

"Sorry." Anna noticed that the explosion of leaves around them was weightless, expanding like a balloon in the air. "Whoa, that's pretty."

"They're turning around again!" Molly shouted from above, where she was tangled in the cords. "Don't they ever stop?"

"They didn't stop coming at me until I was on the ground." Javi stared at Anna. "Not until you . . ."

"Turned the device off," Anna said.

She looked at the glowing machine in her hands. Maybe the birds were attracted to it somehow. Which meant she should turn it off, except—

She looked down at the ground, at least fifty feet below. With normal gravity on, they would all tumble to their deaths.

"Fly to the ground, quick!" Molly unclipped the bungee cord from her belt and kicked off downward from the tree. She pulled her way past branches like a diver descending through seaweed.

Javi managed to unwind himself and followed. But as Anna unhooked the clip from her belt, she realized that a bungee cord was wrapped around her leg. She was roped to the tree, tight.

The shredder birds were drawing closer, their screams rending the air.

"Uh-oh," she said.

"Anna! Get moving!" Molly called from below her, dangerously close to the edge of the device's range.

"I'm stuck." Anna hooked herself to the bungee cord again, then flung her arms around the tree trunk. "Grab on to something in five! Four! Three!"

At *zero*, she turned the device off.

Normal gravity struck, and Anna skidded down the trunk a little. But the bungee cord bit into her leg, jerking her to a halt. She swayed in the air, the narrow treetop sagging under her weight, but she didn't fall.

The birds came shrieking in, but it was like a targeting beacon had been switched off. The flock scattered through the branches, slicing off fronds and leaves, only a few razor-sharp beaks nipping at Anna's arms and face.

A moment later, they had disappeared into the mists again.

She clung to the tree, ignoring the blood seeping from her wounds and the cord squeezing the life from her leg.

"You okay?" Molly called up.

"Fine." Anna's voice sounded calm in her own ears, but her heart was beating hard now. "Can you guys hold on another minute?"

"No problem," Javi called.

A minute sounded right to Anna. She was happy hanging on to this branch for sixty seconds before turning the device back on if it meant the shredder birds were long gone.

"One, one-thousand. Two, one-thousand. Three, one-thousand," she calmly counted.

But her mind was aflame again, her numbness erased by the pulse of danger in her veins.

Weird, how a bunch of birds would be attracted by a machine—especially one that had never existed before. Because a device that bent the laws of science had to be brand-new, right?

"Eight, one-thousand. Nine, one-thousand. Ten, one-thousand," she went on, feeling tingles in her bungee-wrapped leg.

Of course, this whole jungle was pretty much outside the bounds of science. The white sky, the strange birds and plants, the fact that the airplane crashed in a jungle instead of ice and snow.

This place was just as weird as the device.

By the time Anna had finished counting to sixty and was ready to turn the machine back on and drift down to the ground, she had come to a conclusion that she knew was very strange, and yet made perfect sense.

The gravity device and this jungle were connected somehow.

13

Javi

"This sucks." Javi waved at the insects buzzing around his head. "It's even worse than flying."

Molly thwacked away a vine. "No deadly birds, though."

"True." Javi gave the white sky a nervous glance, then checked the branches for dangling snakes.

"If we can figure out what attracts the shredder birds to the device, maybe we can fix it," Anna said. "And go back to jumping."

Javi frowned. "Since when are they called shredder birds?"

"Since they tried to shred you," Anna said.

"But I discovered them!" Javi said.

"*Discovered* them?" Molly asked.

"Well, I saw them first. I should get to name them."

"Okay, what do you got?" Molly was in front, whacking away vines and fronds with a survival knife. Her hair was singed on one side from the flare collision, and she wore a linen airplane napkin tied into a headband to keep the sweat out of her eyes. All that, combined with the knife, made her look like she was in a low-budget pirate costume.

"Um." Javi thought for a moment. Shredder birds *was* a pretty cool name, but it didn't seem fair to have his only shirt ripped up and not get naming rights.

Now he was wearing a button-down salvaged from a random piece of luggage in the hold. It fit perfectly, which only made it creepier that its real owner was dead. Javi wondered how long it would be before they were all wearing dead people's clothing.

That thought sent all the good names for birds from his mind.

"I'll get back to you," he muttered.

"Shredder birds it is!" Molly cried, slashing through a vine hanging in front of her.

"Can I use the knife next, at least?" Javi asked.

"I called next," Anna said.

"Whatever," he said. "But I get to name the next scary thing we run into!"

Molly didn't answer, just gave him a sharp look, like she didn't want to be reminded that there were plenty more scary things out there in the jungle.

But Javi figured there probably were.

At first, leaving camp behind had lifted his spirits. The crashed airplane seemed haunted by the ghosts of all those other passengers, its broken frame a reminder of how badly everything could go wrong. But out here in the deep jungle, Javi had learned one thing: Technology might fail sometimes, but nature didn't care either way.

Nature was also messy, he thought as he clambered over a fallen tree. The trunk was split open down the middle, and things with too many legs skittered around inside.

At least the flying insects were pretty. They glowed a soft Christmas-light blue. Maybe he could put a bunch of them in a jar and make a lantern, like fireflies in summer.

Lanternbugs? Bluebugs?

It would be pretty awesome, arriving home and announcing that instead of winning a robot-soccer championship, he'd discovered a new animal.

Of course, to do that he'd actually have to get home in the first place.

"It's getting louder," Molly said.

For a moment Javi thought she meant the buzz of insects. But then he felt the rumbling beneath his feet. He cupped his ears to place the sound—the waterfall was still straight ahead.

"Yoshi!" Molly called into the jungle.

"He won't be able to hear you," Anna said. "That waterfall's too loud."

"Onward through the bugs!" Javi cried.

Half an hour's march later, the sound of rushing water had grown thunderous enough to make the fronds tremble. Clouds of spray drifted through the jungle like wandering ghosts, chilling to the touch.

The scent of water made Javi thirsty. His bottle had been empty for a while. This rescue mission had taken longer than they'd planned, and he didn't want to think about how worried Oliver would be.

But finally Molly let out a *whoop* and led them forward to a clearing centered around a huge waterfall. It tumbled down out of the mists, crashing into an outcrop of rock. A rippling pool formed beneath the falls.

Javi stepped forward greedily, empty bottle in hand.

"Wait a second." Anna put a hand on his arm, looking around. "This is a watering hole, but there aren't any animals drinking."

"What?" Molly asked. "You think it's poison or something?"

Anna shook her head. "There might be predators around. Watering holes are a favorite place for ambush hunting."

Javi stared at the cool, glittering water. "*Ambush hunting*, seriously? Why does nature have to be such a pain in the butt?"

"It's funny that you think nature cares about your convenience," Anna said.

Javi rolled his eyes. "Yeah, well at least civilization never tries to eat me."

"So what are we supposed to do?" Molly asked. "Just sit here and . . . wait, what's that?"

Javi followed her gaze. In the red vines tangled around the edge of the pool lay a dark blue shape—arms splayed out on the vines. Was that a *body*?

Javi almost cried out, but then he realized what it was. A shirt.

The same color that Yoshi had been wearing.

"Theories?" Molly asked softly, barely audible above the roar of water. "Conjectures?"

"He went for a swim?" Javi suggested.

Molly shook her head. "Then where *is* he?"

Anna shrugged. "Well, either it's safe around here and he went wandering off. Or the local predator took him, and it's already fed. In which case the watering hole should be safe for the rest of the day."

Javi stared at her. "That's cold. Even for you."

But she *was* making a horrible sort of sense, and the shirt didn't look bloody. Not from this far away, in any case.

"I'm going to check it out," Javi said, and set off across the viney floor of the clearing.

As he drew closer, he noticed how neatly the shirt was arranged, like it was laid out to dry. A fancy shirt like that, Yoshi had probably just wanted to wash it. Score one for the no-predators theory.

Plus, nothing short of a T. rex could've taken Yoshi without a struggle, thanks to his sword. Javi looked carefully. No bloodstains.

So where was the guy?

Then Javi saw something in the undergrowth beside his foot, a glimmer of white among the rusty hues. He knelt to look closer and swallowed.

It was a cluster of bones about the size of a finger.

"What?" Molly called. She was making her way over from the edge of the clearing.

"Wait a second." He leaned closer and realized that there were too many bones for a human finger, a whole string of them three inches long.

He pushed aside the undergrowth a little. It was a tiny spine, the size of a mouse's, maybe. Just a random skeleton.

Javi swallowed. No big deal. When animals died in a jungle, nobody buried them.

But then he saw another little spine a couple of feet from the first one. So maybe there *was* a predator around here.

"Um, I think maybe we should . . ."

"Hey!" Molly shouted.

Javi looked up. Halfway across the clearing, her arms out for balance, Molly was struggling to lift her leg, but it was stuck somehow.

Then Javi saw the vines stirring beneath her, as if an army of snakes was swirling around her feet. He leaped up—

—or tried to.

A vine was wrapped around his right wrist, like a rope. He tried to pull away, but it slid tighter, coiling up his arm.

"What is this?" he yelled.

"Don't know!" Molly cried. "Stay off the vines, Anna."

Javi pulled again, trying to use the strength of his legs to uproot the vine. But it was useless. The vine was too strong, and now his ankles were entangled as well!

Then he remembered the flare in his pocket. He grabbed for it with his left hand, pulled it out.

But as he moved, another vine sprang up and coiled around his left wrist.

He struggled. More of the vines were snaking their way up from the undergrowth, wrapping around his waist, his legs. One was slithering toward his neck. He couldn't bring his hands together to tear the top off the flare.

Clearly, whoever had designed this stupid flare hadn't taken predatory vines into account!

Javi leaned his head down and took the tear-away top between his teeth. As he pulled back, a geyser of sparks hit him in the face. Smoke stung his eyes and filled his lungs, but he waved the gout of flame as much as he could . . .

A hissing sound reached Javi's ears, and a smell like burning grass. A moment later, the grip on his left wrist went slack.

He managed to open his tearing eyes and waved the flare at the vines holding his right arm. They shot back into the undergrowth as fast as snapped rubber bands.

"Anna! Throw me your flare!" Molly called.

Waving the gusher of sparks around him, Javi finally managed to gain his feet. But then a single vine came shooting from the ground. It wrapped around his hand and squeezed, as painful as a handshake from one of his weight-lifting cousins. The flare dropped from Javi's grasp and into the undergrowth.

A pulse went through the vines, spreading out from where

the hissing, sputtering flare lay. But the cord wrapped around his hand stayed firm.

"Why won't you *die*?" he cried out, kicking at its roots.

Then, out of nowhere, a flash of metal sliced through the air.

The pressure on his hand was gone, and Javi stumbled back, landing at the edge of the water. Before him stood a shirtless Yoshi, swinging the samurai sword at the thicket of vines. The sword moved faster than Javi could see, whistling in the air, slicing through the leafy strands like they were spiderwebs.

A moment later, the vines had disappeared again.

Yoshi stood there panting, his sword held ready. The smoke from the sputtering flare wreathed through the clearing, roiled by the spray from the falls. Molly stood ready to ignite the flare Anna had tossed her. But nothing moved in the undergrowth.

"Um, thanks," Javi finally said.

Yoshi slowly lowered the sword, his eyes darting from side to side. Then at last he extended a hand.

"I guess we're even now," he said.

Javi frowned as he took Yoshi's hand and pulled himself to his feet.

Then Javi remembered—he'd found the sword in the luggage. "Um, okay. But you're pretty good with that thing."

"Against a plant? Not exactly a challenge." Yoshi inspected his blade. "You're just lucky I came back for my shirt. Tanglevine is tricky if you don't meet it with steel."

"No kidding," Javi said. "And there's also these birds that . . ."

Javi's voice faded. *Tanglevine.*

He let out a soft sigh.

"Cool name, dude."

14

Molly

I t's getting dark," Molly said. "Maybe we should stop here. It's tricky enough flying in daylight."

"It's really just jumping," Anna corrected her.

"Still tricky." Molly glanced at Yoshi, who didn't seem remotely surprised by all this talk of flying. When Anna had demonstrated the gravity device for him, he'd only nodded. Maybe a little thing like antigravity didn't seem strange to the discoverer of tanglevine.

"Hang on," Javi said. "You want to spend the night out *here*?"

Molly nodded. "It's better than crashing through the trees in the dark."

"I'd rather be in the trees than down with the carnivorous vines!" Javi looked accusingly at the undergrowth. "And who knows what else comes out at night in this place?"

"We can't fly blind," Molly said.

Anna nodded in agreement. "Two words: shredder birds. Not fun in the dark."

"That was seven words," Javi said. "And what about the predators down here?"

Everyone looked at Molly.

"We build a fire," she said, trying to sound certain. "That will keep us safe."

She led the four of them to a bare, rocky outcrop. No one wanted to camp anywhere near the thick undergrowth, even with the roar of the waterfall a good distance away. Obviously, the tanglevine hunted near watering holes, but Yoshi had said he'd sensed it before he'd reached the falls.

They collected kindling along the way, and the fire starter soon had it smoldering. The night hadn't turned cold yet, but an open flame seemed to scare off the animals in the place. The ones they'd met so far, anyway.

Maybe the nighttime had a whole new batch of predators.

Molly put that thought aside. What they needed was a way to fly home without being shredded.

"Tomorrow we'll jump lower," she said. "If we stay below the treetops, we can hit the dirt much quicker if the birds appear."

"Sure," Javi said. "But what if the dirt has tanglevine lurking in it?"

Molly didn't answer. She was too busy trying to ignore the food bar in his hand. She was saving her own to eat right before sleep. Living with her mother had taught her that nothing was worse than waking up hungry in the middle of the night.

"I can handle the vine," Yoshi said, and went back to cleaning his sword. He was buffing it with a yellow cloth, the movement hypnotic in the growing firelight. After a solid minute of polishing, he inspected it from all angles, then pulled out a tiny plastic bottle. Squeezing a few drops of oil onto the blade, he began to rub it into the steel.

Molly suddenly understood. "Your sword isn't rustproof."

Yoshi nodded. "It was forged four hundred years ago. Stainless steel wasn't a thing."

"Whoa," Javi said through his food bar. "So you have to clean it every time you use it?"

"Even a speck of moisture could make it rust."

Molly wondered how many drops of oil were in that little bottle. Probably not as many as there were monsters in this jungle.

She wondered when exactly she'd given up on the idea of help arriving, and why. Maybe because a rescue squad of Canadian Mounties didn't fit in with shredder birds and plants that tried to eat you?

Yeah, that was probably it.

When they got back to the plane, how were they going to explain all this to Oliver?

The buzz of the jungle grew louder as the sky darkened, and a few of the glowing blue insects drifted into camp. Molly stared into the black trees, wondering again what new threats were out there. They should make a schedule for keeping watch through the night . . .

But if she brought that up, everyone would go to sleep imagining unknown monsters. None of them would get any rest.

Molly sighed. It was up to her to stay awake—to keep watch without telling the others. She could sleep tomorrow in the safety of the aircraft cabin.

She ran her fingers though her hair. Anywhere else, she would be freaking out, wondering how to get it cut to mask the singed parts. But here it hardly seemed to matter.

"I thought of a way to signal everyone back at camp," Anna said. "To let them know we're okay."

Molly looked up from the fire. "That would be great. Oliver must be worried sick."

"We can signal him." Anna held up a bundle of twigs. "We turn the gravity off, set this on fire, then throw it two thousand feet in the air. Like shooting up a flare."

"That's almost half a mile," Javi said. "How do we manage that?"

"Check it out." Anna stood up and tossed the bundle of twigs straight into the air. She took a few steps, staring up into the darkness, and caught the bundle two-handed as it fell back to earth.

"Maybe twenty feet," Javi said.

"Right." Molly calculated, wishing Oliver was here. "So you're saying low G lets us throw stuff a *hundred* times higher?"

Anna nodded. "From a standstill, I can jump maybe a yard? And we were jumping a few hundred feet at a time. That's a hundred-to-one ratio."

"But we tested the antigravity bubble. It's only about thirty feet across," Molly said.

"*Across*, yes." Anna held up the device. "But the first time I turned it on, Javi jumped way higher than that. The low-G zone might only be thirty feet across, but I think it goes *all the way up*. It's a cylinder, not a bubble."

"Huh . . ." Molly closed her eyes, remembering Javi floating high above the trees, the emergency door tumbling to the ground. "Why would anyone design it that way?"

"Maybe they didn't have a choice." Anna placed a fist over the fire, so that it was lit by the glow. "Gravity comes from the Earth, right? It reaches up like the light from this fire, and pulls us down." She put her other hand underneath, palm out flat, blocking the firelight from her fist. "So maybe that device makes a gravity *shadow*. Everything above it is almost weightless, because it's cut off from the Earth."

Javi let out a groan and fell back onto the stone. "That makes sense, but it also hurts my head."

"But gravity doesn't *shine*—it warps space." Molly shook her head, realizing that everything she knew about relativity came from extra credit questions and TV shows. "Still, I guess it's the same idea."

"How do you guys know all this stuff?" Yoshi spoke up. He had sheathed his sword and was staring at Anna's shadowed fist.

"We don't *know* anything," Anna said with a shrug. "We're just theorizing."

"But we're engineers. We were flying to Tokyo for a robot thing." Molly tried to say it in an offhand way, like Team Killbot flew to Japanese robotics conferences all the time. But Yoshi didn't look quite as impressed as she'd expected.

"Engineers?" he said, then gave a grunt. "Then why hasn't it occurred to you that we might be on a spaceship?"

They all stared at him.

"A *what*?" Molly sputtered.

"Think about it," Yoshi said calmly. "Shielding the gravity from a whole planet would need some serious hardware, and that device is the size of a Frisbee."

"So?" Molly asked.

"So—in a spaceship the gravity is artificial. You don't have to change the laws of physics, you just have to turn something *off*." When no one reacted, Yoshi gave a tired sigh. "In other words, maybe it's not a gravity device at all. Maybe it's just a remote control."

Molly stared, wondering if Yoshi's day alone in the jungle had addled his mind somehow. Or if he'd eaten some kind of psychedelic plant.

He held up his radio. "And I heard something on this. Some kind of transmission."

"Really?" Molly said. "We haven't gotten anything but static."

Yoshi turned his radio on, and the familiar hiss came out. "Me either. But back at the waterfall there was a beeping. A pattern. On a spaceship, there would be a navigational signal, right?"

Molly turned to Javi and Anna, silently appealing for help.

"This place doesn't have any actual sky," Javi said softly. "Just mist."

Anna nodded. "Like someone's trying to hide the ceiling."

Molly stared at them both. "*What?* I mean, yeah, all of this is really weird. But why would there be a *jungle* on an alien spaceship?"

Instead of answering her, both of them looked at Yoshi.

He shrugged. "If you can build a ship big enough, why not put a jungle in it? Plants create oxygen."

"Exactly the right amount of oxygen for humans to breathe?" Molly asked.

"Maybe they made a few adjustments. They clearly don't want to kill us."

"They *don't?*" Molly cried. "Did you miss the part with the carnivorous plant?"

Yoshi spread his hands. "They're testing us. If you kidnapped some local primitives, isn't that what you would do?"

"I wouldn't kidnap people in the first place!" Molly cried. She turned again to Javi and Anna. "Since when do you guys believe in alien abduction?"

Javi shrugged. "Since something grabbed our plane and stuck us in this weird jungle, more or less."

"Molly, a plant tried to eat us," Anna said calmly. "And a *red* jungle? On Earth, almost everything that does photosynthesis is green. It's like these plants evolved under a different sun."

Molly let out an exasperated sigh, wondering when exactly they'd all gone nuts. You had to gather hard data before you came to conclusions. Especially ridiculous ones.

"Listen, Molly, I'm not saying we're on a spaceship," Anna said. "But whatever is going on is at *least* that weird. I mean, do you have a non-weird theory?"

Molly stared into the fire for a moment before answering.

"I think we're on Earth, because we can breathe and the gravity is the same. I think our plane went off course because there was some weird new technology in the hold, and we crashed someplace no one's ever been before. A lost island, or a valley deep in the Amazon, that was never discovered before because it's always covered in mist."

She stood up and looked into the dark sky.

"And I think I can prove it."

Javi rose from the fire and stood beside her. "You think there are stars up there?"

"Yep. Watch this." Molly jumped as hard as she could, straight up. "How high?"

"Um, about two feet?"

Molly nodded. "Sounds right. And with a boost from the rest of you, I bet I could do twice that. Four feet, multiplied by a hundred, should be high enough to get above any mist!"

"But you'll be bird-bait up there," Javi said. "And you won't be able to turn off the device without splatting yourself."

"Not to mention landing on us," Anna added.

"I'll take a flare," Molly said. "It's worth the risk to know *something* about where we are. Otherwise, this place is going to drive us all crazy."

They all stared at her until Javi sighed and said, "Okay, guys. Everyone up."

A few minutes later, Anna, Javi, and Yoshi stood in a tight circle next to the fire. Their hands were interlinked in the middle, like they were ready to give someone a boost over a fence.

Molly put one hand on Javi's shoulder, then rested her right foot carefully onto the six overlapping palms. With her other hand she turned on the gravity device.

The sickening elevator-drop feeling hit her in the stomach, and the fire made a popping noise—a few burning pieces of wood wafted into the air.

Oops, heat rises, Molly thought. But that problem would be solved once she and the device were lofted above the flames. The antigravity effect might go all the way up, but it only extended about fifteen feet in every other direction—including down.

"One . . . two . . . *three*," she cried, and pushed herself up with all the strength of her arms and legs.

The others grunted in unison, and a moment later Molly was hurtling straight up into the night sky. The firelight quickly shrank below, and soon the jungle itself disappeared, wreathed in mist and darkness.

At first, Molly felt suspended in formless space. The only sense of motion came from damp tendrils of wind brushing her face, the air growing cooler as she rose. But soon she realized that the mist was thinning around her. And finally she saw a few pinpricks of light in the inky darkness above . . .

Stars in the night sky. Beautiful and perfect—they weren't on a spaceship after all.

Molly smiled. This was Earth—which meant there was some chance of getting home. She couldn't wait to tell Yoshi that his alien abduction theory was just as silly as it sounded.

But then, as she felt her ascent coming to an end and the long, slow fall beginning, Molly saw something else in the sky. Two things, in fact, close together.

For a moment she thought they were aircraft lights. But they were too big, and one was a crescent shape. And as she fell back into the mists, Molly realized what they were . . .

A pair of moons. One red, one green.

Yoshi

We're on another planet."

Yoshi jolted awake, his eyes opening to a sky without stars.

Had he really heard the murmured words? Or had he been dreaming?

He sat up, shivering in the cold. Looked around.

"Sorry," came a whisper from the darkness.

It was Molly who'd spoken. She'd said the same thing hours ago when she'd floated back to the ground—*we're on another planet*—in the same stunned voice. Now she was sitting up by the dead fire, framed by the pale horizon.

She pointed at the sky.

Yoshi looked up and came fully awake.

At some point the mist had cleared a little. Now the two moons were dimly visible from here on the ground. Close together, red and green, they stared down at him like the mismatched eyes of some vast monster.

"Did you think I was kidding?" Molly whispered. Her smile glimmered in the dark.

Yoshi shrugged. Somehow, teleportation to another planet seemed harder to believe than being taken away on a spaceship. Or at least harder to come back from.

But those were definitely moons in the sky. Plural.

He decided to change the subject.

"Too hungry to sleep?" His own empty belly had been keen and sharp in his dreams. Last night Molly had offered him one of her food bars, but he'd said no. It was his own fault he'd set out to explore the jungle with nothing but a sword.

"Not hungry." She looked at the others, both asleep. "Just nervous about what might be out there. I thought I'd keep watch."

"Alone?" Yoshi shook his head. "You mean, you've been up all night?"

She nodded, looking only half awake.

"Did anything try to eat us?" he asked.

Molly didn't smile, just turned toward the darkness.

"There was a noise."

Yoshi frowned. The jungle was full of noises—the buzz of insects, the flutter of birds, the scampering of small feet through the undergrowth. And always the shushing of wind in the leaves and fronds.

He listened but didn't hear anything beyond the usual ruckus.

"What kind of noise?" he asked.

"Like a foghorn, maybe. Far away."

"You mean, a *ship*?"

She shook her head. "No, an animal. But a really big one."

"Oh." Yoshi patted his katana. "Well, maybe it's big enough to feed eight people."

"Big enough to *eat* eight people, you mean."

Yoshi considered this. "Then it's probably too big to sneak up on us. You should get some sleep. I'll keep watch."

She looked at him a moment, weighing the offer. Like she didn't trust him not to fall asleep.

"I've got stuff to do." He pulled out the piece of tanglevine he'd saved and started to peel the leaves away. It was green, though many of the plants here were red as blood.

Molly just stared at him. "Um, is that what I think it is?"

"Yes. I saved some."

Her eyes widened. "What *for*?"

"To study. I'm pretty sure it's not edible. All muscle." Yoshi had to smile. "I didn't know engineers were so squeamish."

"Anna loves dissecting things." Molly's gaze stayed locked on the dead vine. "But I prefer stuff that isn't squishy. Give me a user manual and numbered parts."

"Ah, you like order. You and my father would get along."

Molly looked up at Yoshi. His words had come out colder than he'd meant them to.

He turned away and added mildly, "Even dead, the vine is very strong. Useful, maybe. I bet it holds more weight than those bungee cords."

"We want stretchy, not strong. We crash into trees a lot."
Molly shuddered. "Also, I'm not wrapping a dead thing around
my waist."

"You never had a leather belt? That's made out of a dead
thing."

"Okay, I'm not wrapping a dead *alien* thing around my
waist."

Yoshi shrugged. "Suit yourself. But I'll hang on to it, just in
case. We might be stuck working with squishy stuff for a
while."

"You're probably right," Molly sighed. "I'm just tired, I
guess."

"Then sleep," he said, but she was already stretching out
on the stony ground. A moment later, her eyes were closed.

Yoshi pulled the rest of the leaves off the tanglevine, then
tied it to his scabbard, which was made of sharkskin. Another
predator, like the vine.

He slid his katana out, inspected the shine on the blade.
Perfect.

There was nothing to do but stare out into the darkness
and listen to the jungle. All together it was a roar, like ocean
waves rumbling in chorus. But each sound had its own little
story—the shriek and flutter of two birds fighting, the skittering of a creature along a branch. Nothing deadly.

But not long before dawn, Yoshi heard something bigger
out there. Something pushing through the trees, making
branches creak and snap.

Something that moved with purpose and strength.

He tensed, hand on the pommel of his sword, eyes aching as he peered into the darkness. Finally, the sounds faded, until he wasn't sure if he had imagined them. It was Molly's fault, for talking about monsters that sounded like foghorns. There was probably nothing out there.

But Yoshi was glad when morning came, and the horizon finally started to turn bloodred.

When the others were finally awake, the four of them tied themselves together—with bungee cords, not tanglevine—and started to jump for home. They followed a rushing stream that ran away from the waterfall, back toward the plane.

It was Molly's idea, a way to find the closest source of fresh water to camp. The glimmer below was easy to spot through the trees, reflecting the white sky. The stream led them on a winding path, but every ten jumps or so, one of them was flung higher to look for the crashed airplane.

It all seemed sensible to Yoshi, and he let the three engineers do their work. They saw everything as a puzzle to be solved, which kept them focused, instead of worrying about the fact that none of them might ever make it home.

They listened nervously for the "shredder birds," like rabbits in an open field. Like prey.

He decided not to tell them about the large beast he'd heard in the night. It would only scare them and had probably been his imagination anyway.

The engineers were wary of the taller trees that sprouted from the jungle. These trees were spindly, soaring up to disappear into the mist, and came in perfectly round clusters. Even weirder, every cluster seemed to be exactly the same diameter.

"That looks designed," Yoshi said to Molly when they landed a few jumps from one of the towering stands of trees.

"I know." She was untangling her bungee cord. "Like a sign of intelligent life, right? I'd love to check them out, but listen."

Yoshi closed his eyes, and deep within the babble of birds and insects he heard a sound that made his skin crawl. It was almost a growl, like pigs grunting.

"Your 'shredder birds'?"

She nodded, and when they jumped again, it was in the opposite direction.

As they soared, Yoshi shook off the creepiness of the shredder sound and went back to enjoying the heady feeling of floating through the misty branches, a sword on his back.

It was like being a warrior in a fantasy. As if all his years of manga, anime, and movies—and the sword training it had inspired—had been in preparation for this place.

Whatever this place *was*. It still felt contained to Yoshi, moons or not. More like a huge starship than a whole world. The mist was a low ceiling overhead, the dense jungle like walls around them. And those neat circles of trees were something from a giant's garden.

But mostly there was that rumble he'd felt from beyond the waterfall. A vast sound, like the roar of space on the other side of a hull.

Though space was silent, wasn't it?

The roar of engines, then.

He had to go back and discover what his radio had picked up, once the whole starvation problem had been solved. Maybe there was a huge transmitter broadcasting to distant stars.

Whether this was a starship, another planet, or whatever, it made the concerns of his father seem so *small*. Calligraphy and grammar. Business etiquette and making money.

None of it compared to *this*—a whole world to explore, monsters and all. Maybe a whole universe.

Did you do anything useful today, son?

Not much. Just learned to fly.

Yoshi had almost forgotten about the shredder birds when they attacked.

An unearthly screaming came out of the mist, and Javi cried out. Anna switched the device off for a split second, then back on, bending their course downward. With a sickening lurch, Yoshi found himself crashing through layers of branches that scratched and slapped. The creek they'd been following loomed below.

When they were only a few feet from the ground, Anna turned off the device again, and they all splashed heavily into the cold, shallow water. Yoshi stood up to gasp for breath, and he saw that his hands were scraped and bleeding.

Above them, the birds went shrieking through the canopy, like a roiling green dragon with a thousand tiny wings.

Los Angeles Public Library

Baldwin H   ch

1/10/2020   .07 PM

- PATRON RECEIPT -
- CHARGES -

1: Item   37244236758851
Title
Due Date: 1/2020

To Ren   www.lapl.org or 888-577-5275

LAPL Reads: Best of 2019
The best books of the year as selected by our staff.
https://www.lapl.org/best-books

--Please retain this slip as your receipt--

Sliced-through fronds floated down, but the birds didn't seem to notice the humans below.

"See that, Yoshi?" Javi said. "They only care about the device. It's like a homing beacon."

"They're alien birds," Anna said. "It's alien technology. They fit together somehow."

Molly shook her head. "But what was alien tech doing on our airplane?"

Yoshi hunkered in the water, watching as the flock coiled away into the sky. They had sounded so angry and fierce, like vengeful monsters.

"Maybe someone stole it," he said.

They all looked at him.

Yoshi sloshed his way to the bank. "That thing wasn't made by us humans, but what if one of us stole it? Like forbidden magic. The aliens wanted it back, so they took the whole plane."

"Okay," Javi said. "So why dump us in an alien jungle full of stuff that wants to eat us?"

Yoshi sighed. These engineers were good at conjectures and theories, but they weren't very good at stories. He suspected they were too coolheaded to understand anger and revenge.

"Maybe they don't care which human stole it," he said. "And they've chosen us to be punished for the crime."

"Seriously?" Molly asked.

"Guys," Javi interrupted. He was pointing at a tree.

Yoshi looked up. There were gouges in the bark, deep

and savage. About twice his height, they made a crude *X* in the tree.

"Okay, weird," Molly said softly. "Would an animal do that?"

"None that I know of," Anna said.

Yoshi took a step closer. Unconsciously, his arm moved in a figure-eight pattern, as if welding a sword to mark the tree.

"What?" Molly asked. "You think a *person* did that?"

He shook his head. "It's too crude. But you know how cats sharpen their claws on scratching posts?"

"That's a pretty big cat," Javi said.

Yoshi looked at Molly, whose eyes widened.

"I heard something last night," she said. "A cry. Something big."

Yoshi nodded. "I heard it, too, moving out in the jungle."

They all stared up at the marks for a while.

"I say we keep moving," Javi finally said.

An hour later, Yoshi spotted the airplane's crash-landing trail.

It was easy to see from a hundred feet up. Miles of sheared-off trees, scattered wreckage, and spilled luggage. So much destruction and mess. He wondered how long it would take for the jungle to swallow it.

To swallow them all.

Yoshi wafted down to the others and pointed. "The airplane's that way. Maybe thirty jumps."

Molly looked down at the glitter of water below. "Let's keep following the stream, see if it gets closer. We got lucky, though. It looks like thirst won't kill us!"

Javi rubbed his belly. "No, that would be hunger. I hope those guys haven't eaten all the pretzels."

Yoshi hoped so, too. It had been a day since he'd eaten. His hunger seemed to change by the hour, sometimes clanging like an alarm in his head, other times settling into a fuzziness that made everything even more unreal.

Anna kept saying that if you had water, it took two weeks to starve. But after only one day, Yoshi was ready to eat one of the bulbous green berries that grew down by the stream. Or kill and roast one of the fat multicolored birds that sounded like crying babies. Even the big green insects with pinecone heads were starting to look tasty.

Yoshi shuddered at the thought. Maybe when the airplane snacks were all gone . . .

"Let's go," Molly said. "We're almost home."

16

Anna

"You *lied* to me!" Caleb cried.

Anna shrugged. "We told you the truth first. But you didn't believe us."

"Yeah, but who would?" Caleb sputtered, giving the device another dubious look. "I mean, an antigravity machine?"

Anna only smiled at him. Caleb couldn't deny it anymore. He'd seen the four of them bounding in from the back end of the plane, where the stream passed within a hundred yards of the wreckage trail.

In a funny way, it was scary how close that stream had been. The jungle was so dense that they might never have found it without the gravity device. They could've died of thirst right here by the plane, waiting for rescue parties that were probably light-years away.

She cradled the device closer. "Well, now you know."

He picked up the spear he'd made—really a long, straight stick with a sharpened end—and pointed it at her. "You guys can't go sneaking off like that. Or stay out in the jungle all night!"

The others didn't respond. They were all too busy wolfing down pretzels and peanuts. Oliver was passing out potato chips, clearly relieved to see them again.

Anna nibbled at an emergency food bar from one of the survival kits. It was unhealthy to eat too fast when you were hungry.

"We found Yoshi and water," she said calmly. "We discovered a carnivorous vine, and figured out that we're on another planet. That's a pretty useful trip."

"Another planet?" Caleb groaned. "Are you guys *kidding* with that?"

Yoshi spoke up from where he stood with Akiko and Kira. "The girls saw the moons, too. This morning, when the mist cleared. They tried to tell you."

Kira held up her drawing pad, and Anna went over to look. She and Javi had woken up after the mists had rolled back in, and hadn't seen the moons at all.

The drawing showed two moons, one crescent, one full. Molly had said they were red and green, but Kira didn't have colored pencils.

"All you saw was lights in the sky," Caleb said. "They weren't moons because we're not on another planet!"

"They looked a lot like moons," Molly said calmly.

"What if they were rescue airplanes? Did you even try to signal them?"

Molly rolled her eyes. "You mean, wave my arms and yell, *Yo, moons, over here*?"

Caleb rubbed his temples, like this was giving him a headache.

"You should hear Yoshi's theory," Anna said. "It's way freakier."

"We don't need theories—we need *food*!" Caleb thrust his crude spear up at the white sky. "And a way to signal those rescue aircraft. We should build a big enough fire that the smoke rises above the mist. Away from the plane, so we don't have to worry about blowing anything up."

Molly shrugged. "A fire might be a good idea, for when night comes."

She glanced at Anna, who was pleased she knew right away what Molly was thinking: *Don't mention the creature with the foghorn voice, or whatever was scratching its claws ten feet up on a tree trunk. Not in front of Oliver.*

Instead, Anna said, "Cooked food is safer than raw. I've got a few ideas about what to try eating first."

"Today?" Javi asked through a full mouth. "Why would we risk eating alien stuff before the Earth pretzels run out?"

"Because," Anna said, "you don't want to be starving when you try your first alien food. It might make you puke your guts up. And you're going to *need* some pretzels to come back from that."

Javi turned pale, and Caleb just walked away, shaking his head.

While Caleb was busy building his signal fire, the others convened at the stream, at a bare spot with no undergrowth for tanglevine to hide in. Kira and Akiko were filling empty water bottles, and Anna stood ready with the plants she'd gathered for the experiment.

There were three piles of berries. The green ones from the bushes along the stream, the blue kind that grew in the undergrowth, and the red ones that were shaped like popcorn.

Hopefully one of them was nutritious, and none was deadly poison.

"It's best to start with berries," she said.

Molly crossed her arms. "Why?"

Anna smiled. It was always fun explaining biology to Molly, who hated squishy stuff.

"Berries are *supposed* to be edible. It's all about reproduction for them."

"Sexy times!" Javi said.

Anna ignored him. "Berries taste good so that animals will eat them. Because then the seeds get carried in a stomach to some new place, and plopped on the ground, along with fertilizer. In other words, fruit is a plant's way of spreading its seeds, while making sure they're covered with nutritious poo."

"Not so sexy after all," Javi said.

Molly nodded. "Nature is weird."

Yoshi was translating for Akiko and Kira, who also looked dubious.

"So plants *want* their fruit to get eaten?" Oliver asked. "Then why are some plants poisonous?"

"To keep certain animals away," Anna explained. "Like, hot peppers have these tiny seeds that get crushed by mammal teeth. Those peppers reproduce better if birds eat them. So they evolved to be too spicy for mammal tongues."

"Because birds *like* spicy food?" Molly asked.

Anna smiled. "Fun fact: Birds don't have taste buds."

"But I'm a mammal," Javi said. "And I *love* hot peppers!"

"That's a kick-butt thing about humans," Anna said. "We eat and drink poisonous stuff for fun."

"True." Javi wore a smirk. "I ate a whole jar of jalapeños once. Let's see a tiger do *that*."

"Tigers have better things to do," Anna said.

Molly was frowning. "So if we avoid stuff that tastes bad or burns our tongues, we should be okay?"

Anna hesitated. In nature, there were lots of exceptions to any rule. Evolution was like a gazillion microprocessors— one inside every living cell—all running slight variations of their DNA code at the same time, seeking out the best results. It was bound to be complicated.

But to keep everyone from starving, she had to make it sound simple. Because sometimes lying was okay.

"If it tastes good, it won't kill you," she said. "If in doubt, spit it out."

Yoshi finished his running translation for the girls, then

asked, "But if this is really another planet, why would *anything* be healthy for us?"

"Because it's all so familiar," Anna said. "There are birds, trees, insects. For everything to wind up looking the same as life on Earth, it has to be made from the same building blocks. As long as the proteins are the same, we can survive."

Yoshi translated this for the girls, but he didn't sound completely convinced. Then again, neither was Anna. Convergent evolution happened all the time on Earth—similar animals emerging from different gene pools, every biome looking more or less the same, from top predators down to bottom feeders.

But on another planet?

All she really knew was that they had to test the theory, or starve. And that she was proud of herself for not saying any of this scary stuff out loud.

But then Oliver said, "So we're *really* on another planet?"

"I guess we can't be sure," Molly said. "But it's the only explanation that fits all the facts."

"So that means we're light-years away from Earth," he said softly. "And we're never getting home."

"No it doesn't!" Molly said. "If we got here, there has to be a way back."

Javi spoke up. "I mean, if someone can teleport us here, or whatever they did, then they can send us back the same way."

Anna tried to think of something to say, but no words came to her. Maybe Javi was right, and some kind of easy-to-use teleporter had brought them here. But what if they'd been shipped here unconscious and frozen, and the trip had taken a hundred years?

What if they'd lost everything already and didn't even know it?

But Oliver only sighed. "Okay, let's eat. Who gets to go first?"

"We choose randomly." Anna held out five straws from the airplane kitchen, then dipped one into the pile of green berries she'd gathered—the same berries the lucky winner was going to eat.

Kira spoke up, and after some arguing, Yoshi translated. "She says you're missing two straws. The girls want to help."

Anna looked at Molly. It was weird enough, having a straw in there for Oliver. But testing possibly poisonous berries on the two young sisters seemed downright wrong. Kira, however, had her fists balled up like she was ready to fight. Even the usually timid Akiko wore a firm expression.

"Sure," Molly finally said, and Anna pulled two more straws from her pocket.

They were all in this together, she supposed.

"It doesn't matter who draws," Javi muttered. "It's going to be me eating those berries. Randomness hates me."

"Randomness treats everyone the same," Oliver said. "That's what random *means*."

"My last words shall be *I told you so*."

"Respect the straws," Oliver said, stepping forward.

Anna stared at him, a little surprised.

Oliver shrugged. "Might as well go first. The odds are the same, and this way I get to stop stressing . . . probably."

As he said that last word, he yanked a straw out of Anna's hand, his eyes wide.

No berry stain.

"Congratulations," Molly said. "But keep that straw. If these berries aren't edible, we're going to keep going till we find some that are."

Oliver's smile faded a little, but Anna was glad he wasn't testing the first batch.

Molly went next. She gazed at the straws for a long moment, muttering, and when she finally pulled one out, it was clean. She looked a little disappointed, like she'd *wanted* to go first.

But again Anna was relieved, even though Molly's safety made her own chances worse. They all needed Molly alive and well.

Of course, Anna didn't want any of them to die. Not any of the younger kids, or Javi, or herself. And *especially* not Yoshi. It seemed wrong for someone with all those sword skills to die of something as weak-sauce as berry poisoning.

"This is a waste of time," Javi said. "It's going to be me!"

Oliver sighed. "You have a twenty percent chance. Same as everyone else who hasn't gone."

"Speaking of people who haven't gone," Yoshi spoke up, "why isn't Caleb here?"

"He'd just get in the way," Molly said.

"But that's not fair," Oliver said.

Molly sighed. "He's in the jungle gathering wood, and he didn't believe us about tanglevine. That's probably more dangerous than eating berries."

"Especially when *I'm* the one who's going to wind up . . ." Javi began, but his voice faded as Kira stepped forward, gazing at the straws.

When she reached out a hand, Anna flinched away. But Kira stared her down, and something about her fierce expression let the numb part of Anna's mind take over. All of them were alive thanks only to random chance. Any of them could be dead in a week. From hunger or from some alien virus. Or from being torn apart by shredder birds or carnivorous vines or something much worse.

Maybe poisonous berries would be an easier way to go.

Anna held out the straws, and Kira took one.

The end was stained green with berry juice.

17

Javi

U h-oh," Javi said.

Kira was gazing at the green-tipped straw. After a long moment, a soft smile curled her lip. Akiko looked like she was about to cry.

Molly stepped forward. "Maybe we should—"

"She's too young," Yoshi said. "I'll do it instead."

Kira must have understood. She let out a burst of angry Japanese and waved the straw in Yoshi's face.

She wasn't backing down. Her white streak of hair flashed in the sunlight.

Javi edged a little closer to the pile of green berries. They looked ripe and sweet, and his taste buds were tired of pretzels.

"Let me," Molly said. "This was all my—"

"You already chose a straw!" Yoshi cut in. He switched to Japanese and started arguing with Kira.

Javi reached for the berries. It was easy, really, because he'd always known it would be him. He was always the loser at rock-paper-scissors or coin tosses, all the way back to his first eeny, meeny, miny, moe. Kira had just gotten in the way of the natural order of things.

Besides, he was really hungry. And those berries did look good.

He picked up three and ate them.

As he chewed, a taste flooded his mouth . . . not a good one.

There was a metallic sharpness to it, like pennies on his tongue. And also a pasty, flowery flavor—ground-up chalk mixed with the contents of his grandma's fancy soap dish. On top of it all, a fierce bitterness twisted up his mouth.

The awful taste must have shown in his expression, because the others fell silent.

Javi started to take a breath, but adding air to the chewed-up berries was a bad move. The smell of rotten eggs filled his head.

His eyes watered, and he felt Molly's hand on his shoulder. "You okay?"

"Spit it out!" Anna cried.

He managed to cough once, and a gob of green flung itself from his mouth. Everyone leaped back, like they expected the berries to come for them next.

But the taste was padlocked to Javi's tongue. Its tendrils were crawling down his throat, making their way toward his stomach. And every time he managed to take a breath, the rotten-eggs smell expanded. His vision went fuzzy, and he felt himself drop to his knees.

"Javi!" Molly cried. "Drink this!"

She waved something—a water bottle—in front of his face, but Javi pushed it away. Water would only carry the acid tendrils farther down his throat.

But they reached his stomach anyway, and it was like a switch was thrown. His whole body lurched, and everything he'd eaten since reaching camp that morning leaped from his stomach. Hot and salty, it streamed up his throat and into his mouth, then out through his lips and onto the ground.

Two more gigantic heaves came from him, emptying his stomach completely. A moment later, Javi found himself curled up in the dirt, gasping and clutching his belly.

"Um, are you okay?" Molly asked from about ten feet away.

Javi didn't answer. The thought of his abdominal muscles flexing again, even to push out a single word, was too much.

But the weird part was, he didn't feel that bad.

He felt clean inside. His vision was sharp, his eyes washed by tears. Even his sinuses were clear. The half-digested airplane pretzel smell that filled the clearing was particularly crisp, if not very pleasant.

"I'll live," he whispered.

"Whoa," Anna said. "That was fast. It was like those berries were *designed* to make you puke." Anna knelt beside him, looking into his eyes. "Your pupils look normal, as far as I can tell. This is kind of perfect."

Javi stared at her. "Um, which definition of *perfect* are you using? Because I give those berries one star."

"Sorry. It sucks to barf. But this is exactly what we need for food testing!" She looked up at Molly. "If anyone gets sick, we can use the green berries to flush them out. It's like having a stomach pump on call!"

"Just what I've always wanted." Javi sat up and reached for a water bottle.

Kira knelt down in front of him, staring into his eyes. She reached out . . . and flicked his nose.

"Ouch," Javi said. "What was that for?"

She said something in Japanese.

Yoshi smiled. "She says wait your turn and don't play the hero. But I think you were brave." He bowed.

Before meeting Yoshi, Javi had never seen anyone bow, except maybe as a joke. It seemed somehow formal and heartfelt at the same time. "Thanks."

"Kira says she'll go next," Yoshi announced to the group. "And I'll go after her."

"I feel like the straws aren't being respected," Oliver said.

Molly sighed. "Maybe random chance *isn't* the best way to make decisions. I'll go after you guys."

"Not necessary, Molly," Anna said. "We only have two more kinds of berries. But the rest of you don't have to worry. There'll be plenty of other weird stuff to try. We haven't tried eating a bird yet, and those big green insects might be a good source of protein. You might envy Javi by the time this is all over."

"I wouldn't go that far." Javi stood up. His legs were a little shaky, and his mouth tasted bad. The grandma's-soap-dish taste had been washed away, but the tang of stomach acid was still there. He tried not to look at the puked-up airplane pretzels on the ground.

He stumbled to a rock and sat down heavily.

Yoshi gestured to Kira, indicating the other piles of berries—blue and red. She leaned close to inspect them, giving each a sniff.

After a moment, Kira picked up a few of the red berries, closed her eyes, and popped them in her mouth.

She chewed a few times, then opened her eyes.

"Omoshiroi," she said.

"Interesting," Yoshi translated.

Javi leaned back and took a sip of water. *"Omoshiroi,"* he repeated. That was one Japanese word he figured he would always remember.

Kira ate another handful of the red berries and shrugged. She rubbed some of the juice into the white streak in her hair, and it instantly stained red.

She smiled at this, and Akiko gathered her into a hug.

"My turn," Yoshi said.

He approached the blue berries and picked one up. After a deep breath he cautiously ate one, then another.

"Whoa. These are really good." He reached for more, a sudden look of hunger in his eyes.

"Not too many," Anna said. "You guys should wait a couple of hours, just to make sure there's not some kind of slow-acting poison in them. The moment you start feeling weird, eat one of Javi's berries to get rid of everything inside you."

"They aren't called *Javi's berries*," Javi said. "As their discoverer, I do not permit that!"

Anna laughed. "Okay, so what are they called?"

Javi thought for a moment. "From now on, they shall be known as . . . pukeberries."

Everyone nodded in agreement, and Javi took another sip of water and closed his eyes.

His work here was done.

18

Yoshi

I t still counts, Kira," Yoshi said. "Even if you don't vomit."

"Stay still." Kira looked up from her sketch pad and frowned at his pose. While they waited to see if the berries they'd eaten were poisonous, she was drawing him.

"I hope that boy is okay," Akiko said.

"Ha-bi," Yoshi sounded out. Javi's name didn't quite work in Japanese, but it was close enough.

"He was annoying," Kira said. "He stole my glory."

Yoshi laughed, but Kira silenced him with a dark look. He went back to his pose—gazing up at the crashed plane in wonder, a hand on the hilt of his sword.

"Vomiting didn't *look* very glorious." Akiko glanced at the airplane-sheared tree trunk beside her, where a pile of green pukeberries sat in case of medical emergency.

"We won't need those," Yoshi reassured her. "Please, play some more."

Akiko smiled and picked up her flute again. Well, it wasn't really hers—she'd found it stowed in the flight attendants' closet. Her own instrument was probably somewhere in the trail of wreckage behind the plane.

She began to play something slow and soft, and Yoshi let the music soothe his nerves. Waiting around like a lab rat was bad enough, but posing like this was just humiliating.

He was also dizzy from hunger. By now it was clear that Kira's *interesting*-berries weren't deadly, and the blue berries he'd tried were not only safe, but delicious. Yoshi wanted to eat a thousand of them, but he'd promised Anna to wait until sunset before eating more.

Sunset.

He tightened his grip on his katana, remembering the sound he'd heard last night—the huge body lumbering through the jungle. After Javi had spotted those gouges in the tree trunk today, Yoshi was less certain that it had all been in his imagination. Didn't some predators only hunt at night?

As the shadows lengthened, the noises of the jungle seemed to come alive.

"How long will your drawing take?" he asked.

The scratch of Kira's pencil didn't pause. "As long as it takes."

Akiko looked up, shrugging an apology as she played.

"We're wasting time," Yoshi said. "We have food and water now. We should be trying to *understand* this place."

Akiko stopped playing. "Do you really think we're on another planet?"

"You saw the moons," Kira said.

"They could've been weather balloons," Akiko said. "Or rescue planes, looking for us!"

"That's what Caleb thinks." Yoshi looked around. "But this jungle, these animals—none of it looks like Earth. And the waterfall that feeds our stream, there's something behind it."

Kira stopped drawing. "What do you mean?"

"I heard a sound on my radio out there. Just beeps, but it had a pattern." He closed his eyes, trying to remember. "And I *felt* something, too—a trembling in the ground, in the air. Some giant process at work. This place isn't still. It's moving, changing around us."

When he opened his eyes, Kira was still staring at him.

"Interesting," she said.

Apparently, that was her favorite word. She had worked more of the *interesting*-berries into the bleached lock of her hair, and now it shone a luminous red.

"I'm going to go back to the waterfall," Yoshi said. "And past it, to see what's out there. We can't sit around waiting for this place to eat us!"

Kira frowned. "But if you get lost, we won't have a translator."

"How inconvenient for you."

"I'm only saying, your Japanese *is* very good."

Yoshi felt his spine stiffen. "I was born in Tokyo."

"But you're a half, aren't you?"

"My mother is American," he mumbled.

Kira nodded, as if all her suspicions had been confirmed.

Yoshi resumed his pose, mastering his expression as he turned back to the crashed plane. He was used to this—being a curiosity, an oddity, a threat to logic and good sense. He would always be the foreigner who spoke Japanese too well, who wasn't quite foreign *enough*. It made people nervous, the way he didn't fit in one box or the other.

He wondered if Kira was drawing his face differently, now that she was certain.

"Do you miss them?" she asked.

"My parents?" He shrugged. "My mother and I had a fight just before I left. And my father and I were about to have one when I arrived in Japan."

Kira shook her head. "Poor Yoshi-chan. Is that why you're so broody?"

He ignored her. The strange thing was, he hadn't thought much at all about home. On the plane, he'd already missed his life back in New York, but that seemed a hundred years ago now.

Why would he want to sit around talking about manga when he was *living* in one?

"What about your parents?" he asked.

"We haven't seen them in a month," Akiko stopped playing to say. "We were in a Swiss finishing school, learning how to behave properly."

Kira rolled her eyes. "A punishment for me. A reward for her."

"I loved it!" Akiko said. "We learned all about air kisses and protocol, and we spoke French the whole time!"

"We learned about table settings," Kira grumbled. "So many forks."

Akiko was about to say more, but a bird fluttered into view and settled above them on the wing of the plane. It opened up its mouth and sang, a rising note with a little trill at the end. It was one of the slide-whistle birds, as Anna called them— the only ones here that sounded like they belonged on Earth.

Akiko played her own trill on the flute, a little higher in pitch than the bird's song. It cocked its head, listening.

"Almost," Yoshi said.

Akiko played the trill once more. This time she matched the bird's song perfectly.

Yoshi smiled encouragement. Maybe that flute would be useful. Didn't duck hunters use calls to lure their prey closer?

His fingers shifted on his sword hilt.

Kira was watching him, and spoke softly. "The others will be too afraid to explore with you."

"They've already been out to the waterfall."

"Only to look for you."

Yoshi kept his eyes on the bird. "They're engineers. They're curious."

"Engineers aren't curious," she said. "They're *cautious*. That's why bridges don't fall down. Mostly."

Yoshi had to smile at that. It was true that Molly always demanded a long discussion before any decision was made. She wanted *theories* and *conjectures*. What would it take to convince her that they needed to go out into the jungle again, where unknown monsters lurked? To search beyond the waterfall for whatever was sending out radio transmissions? To investigate the perfectly circular stands of trees, even if there were shredder birds in the way?

Yelling drifted in from the jungle. The others were helping with Caleb's signal fire, which no one would ever see. Yoshi sighed—more time wasted.

Unless that foghorn creature was afraid of fire. That was probably why Molly was helping him.

The slide-whistle bird fluttered down from the wing and alighted on the sheared-off trunk. It stared at Akiko curiously.

"You'll need the gravity machine to explore," Kira said. "They won't let you borrow it. Because you ran off alone and had to be rescued."

"They didn't rescue me—I rescued *them* from tanglevine. And I was the one who found the source of our water."

"They don't see it that way."

"How do you know? You can't even understand what they're saying."

Kira shrugged. "I don't have to know English to understand them. They think they're smarter than everyone else. That's why they talk everything to death."

Yoshi couldn't argue with that.

The bird fluttered closer, and Akiko paused to giggle at it.

"Keep playing," Kira whispered. She glanced at Yoshi's sword hand and gave him a half smile.

Akiko played the trill again, and this time the bird answered. It hopped along the trunk toward the pukeberries. Almost within reach.

The smell of smoke wafted in from the jungle, along with some cheers. Caleb's signal fire was burning at last.

Of course, a fire could be useful . . . for cooking.

Yoshi eased the katana halfway out of its scabbard. The freshly oiled metal made no sound, and the bird was interested in the pukeberries now. Akiko's eyes were closed as she listened to its song.

The felled tree was old wood, hard as iron. But if he swept across it, a horizontal *suihei* cut just like in practice, he could strike without damaging his blade.

The bird hopped closer to the berries—it bent down to peck at them.

In one motion, Yoshi drew his sword and struck. The katana flashed sideways through the air. Feathers flew as the bird shrieked and fluttered for a moment toward the sky. But a second later it tumbled down and hit the ground, where it bounced and jittered like oil in a hot pan, blood spraying. Akiko dropped the flute, her scream mixing with slide-whistle cries.

Yoshi stepped forward, caught the fluttering tail under one foot, and drove the point of his katana through the bird and into soft dirt.

An endless moment later, it stopped moving.

Akiko started crying, and Kira jumped up and held her tight.

"Sorry," Yoshi said. He hadn't meant to scare Akiko. But this bird was food.

It was survival.

Kira kept her arms wrapped around Akiko's shoulders, but smiled up at him.

Yoshi sighed and pulled his sword free. The blood on the metal and the ground was red, just like an Earth creature's blood. Maybe Anna was right, and these creatures weren't too alien to eat.

Smoke was drifting from the jungle now, and the smell made Yoshi even hungrier. He picked up the bird by one limp wing and headed for the building crackle of the fire.

This was how you survived. Not with theories and conjectures. You caught your dinner by swinging a blade, not arguing. And you cooked it on the same fire that protected you from monsters.

Yoshi was going to find out what was behind the waterfall, whether the others wanted to come or not. Even if it meant stealing the gravity device.

"Yoshi-chan!" Kira called, and he spun around.

Kira still had a protective arm around her sister, but with her free hand she held out a few pukeberries.

"Just in case the meat's poisonous?" she said gently.

The bird gave a last flutter in his hand, and Yoshi almost dropped it. How was it still alive?

He walked back to take the berries.

19

Molly

"Missed again." Molly wafted back to earth, her improvised net fluttering in the breeze.

"It's weird." Anna settled into the undergrowth a few yards away. "It's like those birds *know* how to fly in low G."

"Nets are pointless," Caleb said for the dozenth time. "We should just throw stuff at them."

Molly frowned, watching the latest slide-whistle bird flutter away uncaught. When it reached the edge of the device's range, its wingbeats shifted into normal-gravity flight without the slightest hitch.

How did a *bird* know how to deal with a gravity distortion field?

"Get ready for heavy," Anna said, and switched off the device.

Molly's stomach lurched, her feet sinking into the soft ground. She was tired, her muscles sore, and her clothes smelled like smoke. Maybe it was time to give up.

But Yoshi's slide-whistle bird had tasted so *heavenly*. The smell of it roasting by the bonfire had made everyone— except Akiko—volunteer to try it first. In the end they'd all risked eating it together, because no one wanted to wait.

Molly had only allowed herself a small piece, which had burnt pieces of feather stuck to it. But after two days of pretzels and food bars, the taste of fresh meat was amazing.

"Hunger makes the best sauce," Javi had proclaimed. "Though I have to say, *omoshiroi*-berries also make a pretty good sauce."

It was true. Kira's red berries were tangy and crisp, like tiny bitter oranges. The perfect complement to slide-whistle meat.

But they'd spent the rest of the daylight trying to catch another bird and failing, and darkness had snuck up on them. The jungle around the clearing was full of mysterious noises and shadows now. Anything could be out there, watching them flail at birds.

Molly wondered if they should spend the night out here, protected by the bonfire. Or was it safer back at the plane?

Caleb hefted his spear. "Just stand back and give me space, guys. I can't miss!"

"You already missed four times," Oliver said tiredly.

"Yeah, but I'm nailing the next one!"

"You can't catch them without Akiko," Yoshi called.

Everyone looked up at him and the two girls. They were up the hill, next to the bonfire. Kira looked amused by their efforts, but Akiko was watching with an unhappy expression, her flute silent by her side.

Molly led the others back up. "You said she didn't want to help."

Yoshi shrugged. "Another day of berries and pretzels might change her mind."

"Just what we need: a pied piper with a conscience." Molly realized that she was hungrier now than before she'd eaten her one bite of bird. One successful hunt didn't solve all their food problems.

She looked at the gravity device in Anna's hand. "You don't suppose one of those symbols is for bird-zapping, do you?"

Anna's eyes lit up. "You want to experiment?"

It was tempting, but Molly shook her head. Between taste-testing alien berries and cooking a bird for the first time, she'd had enough trial and error for one day.

Besides, the sun had set. She had to stay watchful.

"It's too dark to mess with the laws of physics."

"Right, and the bonfire's starting to burn down." Caleb stuck his spear into the ground and looked up into the misty sky. "We've got to build it back up. This is the best time for a rescue plane to spot us."

Molly rolled her eyes at Anna.

Caleb saw it. "I know. You still think this is another planet. One of those alien worlds that has breathable air and plenty of stuff to eat!"

"As opposed to some hidden island full of alien wildlife?" Molly asked. "Where radios and compasses don't work, and there's antigravity technology lying around?"

Caleb didn't answer, just gave the device in Anna's hands a dirty look.

Then Oliver spoke up. "What's the difference?"

Everyone stared at him. He stared back, his jaw set.

"What do you mean?" Javi asked gently.

"You all act like *that's* the big question," Oliver said. "Is this a planet? A spaceship? A hidden island? But wherever it is, we're here and five hundred other people aren't! So where *are* they?"

Nobody said anything, and the night noises of the jungle rushed in to fill the silence.

Molly felt her hunger joined by another emptiness. An absence she had tried to crowd out of her mind with theories and conjectures.

"We don't—" she began.

But Anna interrupted, her voice emotionless. "When the electricity came into the plane, it was analyzing us. Testing us. It chose us eight, and no one else."

"Okay," Oliver said. "So someone brought us here. *What did they do with everybody else?* Isn't that the real question? The one you're all afraid to ask?"

He paused, his fists balled in defiance. The fire crackled in the cooling night air.

"Because they're all dead," he finally said.

Molly shook her head, trying to ward off the words. "We don't really know what—"

"You *do* know. You're just afraid to say it! You think I'll start crying and freaking out." Tears ran down Oliver's face, but his fists stayed clenched. "And that just makes it *worse*!"

Molly stepped back from him. "What does?"

"Not talking about it!" Oliver took a deep, shuddering breath. "We should say something about Mr. Keating at least. I mean, he was our *friend*. Without him we wouldn't even know each other. But you guys are too chicken to admit he's dead, and you're pretending it's *my* fault!"

The members of Team Killbot all looked at one another, and when Molly saw Javi's guilty expression, she knew exactly what Oliver meant.

As usual, it was Anna who said the uncomfortable truth out loud.

"You're right. We didn't want to face it, and we used you as an excuse. Sorry, Oliver."

He stared at her a moment, then nodded. "Don't apologize. Just say it."

"It's true," Javi said, looking like he'd just woken up. "They're all dead. And we should say something about Mr. Keating."

Molly tried to swallow the stone in her throat—this was all

her fault. It had worked on the plane, distracting Javi from his fears. But when five hundred people were dead, you didn't hide it with trivia questions.

Of anyone, she should have known better. After Molly's father had died, her mother never talked about him, until she'd gotten so good at silence that now she never talked at all.

And Molly had tried to do the same thing to Oliver.

"I'm sorry." She took a deep breath. "And I'm sorry I talked your mother into letting you come, Oliver."

He managed a smile. "You didn't know the plane was going to crash."

Molly shrugged. Sure, it was a one-in-ten-million chance. But it was her responsibility to make it right if she could. That's what being the leader meant.

"Okay," she said. "Mr. Keating . . . He was a really cool guy. He taught us how to be engineers, and how to think for ourselves. And he might be gone, but he's why Team Killbot is going to make it through this."

She looked at Javi, who cleared his throat.

"I didn't really have friends at school before you guys," he said. "I used to feel sick every Sunday night, because Monday morning came next, and it always felt so lonely. But now I look forward to school. I have Mr. Keating to thank for that."

Oliver spoke up next. His voice was at the edge of breaking, and it sounded like he'd said the lines already a hundred times in his head. "He showed me that math can make robots.

- 138 -

Before that, I thought I was totally uncool. Now I'm not so sure."

Oliver looked like he wanted to say more, but his tears were running freely now.

Molly glanced at Anna, hoping she didn't feel forced to speak. Sharing really wasn't her strong point, especially at moments like this, when it was easy to say the wrong thing.

But Anna took a breath. "He let me be the way I am. He made it a puzzle to be solved, instead of something wrong with me."

Molly swallowed, letting the noises of the jungle fill the clearing for a while. Finally, she knuckled away the tear rolling down her own cheek and faced Caleb. He was turned toward the airplane, looking embarrassed and bored.

But this had to be hard for him, with no friends in this strange place. Maybe it was time to let him contribute. Part of Molly hoped he was right and she was wrong, so maybe they could all still get home.

"Do you really think this is Earth?" she asked.

"Of course it's Earth," Caleb said, still not looking at the rest of them. "We aren't freezing to death or boiling away. And no one's ever discovered an exoplanet the right distance from its sun to support human life."

Molly blinked. "An exoplanet?"

"That's a planet in another solar system."

"I know what it means, but since when did you get all Mr. Science?"

Caleb snorted. "Since I got my first telescope, when I was ten. Playing with toy robots doesn't make you the only people who know stuff."

A few rejoinders went through Molly's head—that the Killbots weren't toys, any more than the robots that defused bombs or built cars or rescued people after earthquakes were. But she found herself with a smidgen of newfound respect for Caleb.

She looked at the others. They were all listening, happy to replace grief with something else to think about. Anything else.

"So you know astronomy," she said. "If you saw the stars, could you figure out if we're on Earth or not?"

"That's easy. I even could tell you *where* on Earth we are—or at least the latitude." He looked up. "But the mist makes it impossible."

"What if we got you *above* the mist?" Molly asked with a smile.

Caleb's eyes widened. "You mean, with that gravity thing?"

"Flying is the bomb," Anna said.

Caleb didn't answer for a moment.

"You can help us figure out where we are," she said.

He finally let out a sigh. "Okay. I'll fly up and check out the stars, but only if you help me build the fire back up first. Just in case we *aren't* on an alien planet and there are people looking for us."

"It keeps the bugs away," Molly said with a shrug.

Then she realized that she was doing it again. Keeping the truth from the others, when they needed to know what was going on if they were going to survive.

"It probably keeps the monsters away, too," she added softly. "Let's stoke the fire."

20

Javi

Bonfires were easy when you could turn the gravity down.

Javi had to admit, Caleb had picked a good spot for his signal fire. It was a half mile back along the debris trail, far away from any leaking jet fuel. Here, the belly of the descending aircraft had clipped a small hill, knocking a dozen trees out of the ground to create a clearing. The trees were too big to carry in normal gravity, but in low G each weighed no more than a box of schoolbooks.

Javi, Caleb, and Molly found a knocked-over tree in the darkness, then Anna turned down the gravity. While they carried the fresh log back, the timbers in the fire eased up into the air, carried by the updraft of their own flames.

"Get ready for heavy!" Anna called when the log was in position.

Full gravity returned, and the timbers went crashing down, spitting sparks as oxygen rushed into the fresh spaces created.

A wave of heat billowed out across the hill, and Javi smiled. It was like having a giant poker that stirred the signal fire at the push of a button.

If only there were someone to signal.

It hit him hard, there in the darkness—if they were on an alien planet, all alone, the monsters out there in the dark would always be there. But if Caleb was right and this was Earth, maybe there was hope.

Javi looked up at the sky. No rescue planes rumbled above the roar of the fire and the buzz of insects.

He sighed and bent down to pick up the water bottle full of glowflies—his best name so far. He'd been collecting them all afternoon. One day, their flashlights were going to run out of juice.

"Okay, Astronomy Boy," Molly said. "It's time to go up there and tell us what constellations you see."

Caleb only nodded. Javi wondered if his bossy attitude was fading because he saw how well Team Killbot functioned as a group.

"So I'm just supposed to jump?" he asked.

Molly nodded. "We're already on this hill. With a boost from us, you'll go a few hundred feet up. That'll clear the mist easy."

"Sounds like a long way to fall back down."

"It doesn't matter how far you fall," Oliver spoke up, his

eyes still red but his voice steady. "You weigh so little, your terminal velocity is almost nothing."

Caleb crossed his arms. "My *what*?"

"He doesn't mean *terminal* in a bad way," Javi said, grinning.

"Everything has a maximum falling speed," Oliver explained. He picked up a feather left behind from the bird roasting, and let it spiral to the ground. "With the gravity turned way down, your terminal velocity is like this feather's— too slow to hurt you."

"But you can't drop the device." Anna held it up. "And *don't* touch any of these buttons. Unless you want normal gravity coming back when you're three hundred feet up."

"I'm not stupid," Caleb said. He looked ready to go, confident.

Too confident, Javi thought.

"And if you hear a sort of growling?" Javi said. "Those are shredder birds. That's bad."

Caleb stared, like he thought Javi was kidding.

Molly handed him a flare. "If you get into any trouble, light this."

Javi, Yoshi, Anna, and Molly did the honors, gathering around Caleb and interlocking their palms. He was finally looking the right amount of scared, Javi thought, for someone about to be launched hundreds of feet into the air for the first time.

"Get ready for weightless," Anna said.

She switched on the device and handed it to Caleb, and the wafty feeling of low G filled Javi's body. Kira and Akiko took each other's hands.

"Three, two, one, *launch*," Molly cried, and with a grunt they sent Caleb skyward. As he and the device disappeared into the dark mists above, normal gravity settled over them all again.

"I wonder if that thing's battery will ever run out," Javi said, picking up his jar of glowflies. "I mean, does it even *have* a battery?"

"I'm more worried about him landing in the bonfire," Oliver said. "Or would the rising hot air push him back up?"

Molly stared at them. "Did you guys worry about this stuff when it was *me* going up?"

"We trust you to improvise." Javi looked up. "Caleb, not so much."

"We should build some kind of portable engine," Anna said. "We could us those little fans on the—"

"Wait," Molly whispered. "Listen."

A sound was building around them—an ominous rushing sound that made the small hairs on Javi's arms tingle. It seemed to come from the sky, the trees, everywhere.

"Is it getting colder?" Anna asked.

Javi nodded. A chill had wrapped itself around him, and the trees began to stir.

"This is one we didn't think about," he said. "A storm!"

They all looked into the sky again. Caleb was up there somewhere, a kite without a string.

Molly knelt and grabbed some fronds, tore them up, and threw them high into the air. They caught the wind and drifted back along the wreckage trail, away from the crashed plane.

"He's getting blown that way," she called, pointing.

After a moment of silence, Javi flung out an arm. "There!"

"Clever boy," Anna said. "He lit the flare."

In the distance, a tiny red dot was descending. It brightened as it dropped down out of the mists, blazing in the darkness. But a moment later it had disappeared, fallen softly into the thick and unforgiving jungle.

At that moment, another sound rose up in the distance. It was a huge and mournful cry, as deep as a foghorn.

"That didn't sound like a storm," Javi said.

"Omoshiroi," Kira said.

21

Caleb

rilliant," Caleb muttered to himself. "Why did I listen to those *kids*?"

The cold wind stirred the branches around him, pushing him down a few feet toward the jungle floor. He was about halfway between the ground and the canopy, tangled in vines, a flare sputtering in one hand, the gravity device in the other.

Caleb sighed. Weighing nothing had a disadvantage they hadn't mentioned—one sudden wind and he was miles away from where he'd started!

He didn't even know how to turn the device off.

Not that he wanted to at the moment. The jungle below was lit only by the pale blue of the glowflies. The others had warned him about a carnivorous vine down there. That didn't seem likely, but neither did anything else that had happened over the last two days.

Also, when he'd been up there above the mist, Caleb had *thought* he'd heard some kind of animal cry down below.

Maybe staying up here in the trees was better for now.

First things first—he needed a free hand to grab branches, but he couldn't drop the hissing flare. It was his only source of light, and hadn't Molly said that the shredder birds were afraid of fire? Maybe whatever had let out that cry was, too.

Clutching the gravity device between his knees, Caleb managed to pull his belt loose. Working carefully, he used it to strap the device to one shoulder.

Okay. Falling to his death was no longer a possibility. One less thing to worry about. Of course, his pants might fall down at any moment, but that seemed like a fair trade.

With his free hand, Caleb pulled himself weightlessly upward through the flare-lit darkness, until finally the misty sky appeared above.

He pushed off from the treetops, drifting up into the cool wind.

There was the bonfire in the distance. He could just make out a smaller flame off to the side, waving back and forth.

They'd made a torch to signal him with!

Caleb had to admit—those kids weren't completely useless.

He waved the flare back at them, wishing he could send some kind of signal. Something that would tell them what he'd seen in the sky—

Those two moons that *couldn't* be moons. Sure, their light was steady, not twinkling like a star's, and Caleb's sharp eyes had made out craters on their surfaces. But the red moon was almost full while the green one was only a slim crescent—and they were *right next to each other.*

Even on an alien planet, two moons in the same part of the sky would have to be in the same phase, right? Unless the solar system had two suns.

But that didn't make sense, either. Why would each moon only reflect one sun? And then he'd seen something that had removed all doubt . . .

Treetops brushed his feet. He was drifting back down into the canopy, and the wind had pushed him even farther away from the bonfire.

Caleb gave a last wave with his flare, then grabbed for a passing branch. He had to get organized and start making his way back toward the bonfire. This flare wouldn't burn forever, and he definitely didn't want to bounce around this jungle in pitch-blackness.

He got his feet under him. If those kids could jump across the treetops, so could he.

With a grunt, Caleb pushed off as hard as he could. A moment later he was in the air, the jungle passing beneath him.

But he'd angled himself too high. The cool wind caught him head-on, stalling his momentum and making the flare sputter in his hand. By the time he drifted back down into the trees, his forward flight had slowed to nothing.

Caleb grabbed on to the thickest branch he could see and gathered himself for an even harder push.

Yes! This time he had it right. He was sailing just above the trees, straight ahead. To reduce wind resistance, he straightened out and put his hands in front of him. Like a diver going into the water.

No, like Superman!

The flare crackled in his hand, spitting back into his face. Caleb imagined the glittering trail of sparks behind him and smiled through gritted teeth.

Anna was right—flying was the bomb.

Too bad they only had one of these devices. Anna was going to want it back when he returned to camp, wasn't she? The most amazing technology he'd ever seen, and Caleb had let a bunch of kids play around with it.

He wasn't going to make that mistake again.

His next push carried him too high, and the wind caught him once more.

Caleb swore. He needed to focus on jumping. He could decide later who got to keep the gravity device.

A half-dozen jumps later, he noticed something odd. About a hundred yards to his right was a dark space in the jungle. A low spot in the canopy, as if someone had cut off the tops of all the trees. For some reason, the ever-present blue shimmer of glowflies was missing.

Squinting, Caleb saw that the darkness formed a circle about twenty yards across.

He let himself drift to a stop, keeping his eyes on the dark area as he descended. The circle was so exact, it seemed unnatural.

Was it a camp of some kind?

Caleb felt a wariness come over him. If anyone lived out in this weird jungle, he didn't necessarily want to meet them in the dark of night. Alone.

But he was more than halfway back to the bonfire, only a mile from the others. They needed to know about this. He had to take a look.

He pushed carefully through the treetops, not flying up into the cold wind. In a few soft jumps he reached the edge of the dark circle.

The trees were different here. Shorter and stumpier, like a whole new species. Maybe this wasn't a camp at all, just some weird natural formation. Maybe the darkness was only because glowflies didn't like this kind of tree.

But why were they growing in an exact circle?

And hadn't Molly said something about circular stands of trees farther out in the jungle? But those were taller, not shorter . . .

It was only twenty yards across. He could zoom all the way with one push, keeping his eyes open the whole way.

Caleb steadied himself and shoved off gently.

As the perfect circle of darkness opened up below him, his stomach lurched a little.

No, his stomach was lurching a *lot*.

From his shoulder, the gravity device let out an annoyed little buzzing sound. Like an alarm clock, insistent and pulsing.

"Uh-oh," Caleb said.

With awesome suddenness, gravity jerked back into existence around him. His full weight came crashing down like a blanket of lead, and a moment later he was falling . . .

Hard.

22

Anna

"id anyone else see that?" Molly asked.

Anna didn't answer, just kept her eyes locked where the flare had arced suddenly down, like a shooting star dropping from the sky.

It didn't reappear. She saw nothing but dark trees shivering in the wind.

"Theories?" Molly prompted. "Conjectures?"

"He could've hit something," Javi said. "He's never jumped before."

Yoshi shook his head. "It went down too fast. He probably just dropped the flare."

"Or maybe he ran into whatever creature made that noise," Anna said.

Everyone stared at her, but she ignored them, gazing into

the blackness. Was there something different about the spot where Caleb had disappeared?

Maybe it was just her eyes playing tricks on her, but the trees seemed a little darker there. The blue glimmer of the glow-flies was missing.

"Maybe the device's batteries ran out," Javi said quietly.

Anna frowned. She was worried about Caleb, but also couldn't escape the feeling that it was *her* gravity machine out there, maybe lost now. Why had she handed it over to a noob?

"No, Yoshi's right. That was the flare going down, not him." Molly rubbed at her singed hair. "He must have burned his hand and dropped it."

"Then he'll fly down and pick it up," Anna said, and shivered. "Since when are jungles freezing?"

"The water at the falls was cold, too," Yoshi said.

Anna looked at him. "We should check that out."

Molly sighed. "We're not going anywhere until Caleb brings us back our gravity device. Do you guys see *anything*?"

Silence fell over them, except for the crackle of the bonfire and the low moan of moving air. The mists were clearing a little, parted by the wind. The soft light of the moons began to color the sky, and patches of moonlight swept across the jungle.

No one said anything as they watched and waited.

Then Anna saw it—a pale trickle of smoke drifting up from the spot where Caleb had disappeared. The trees there *were* darker, she was certain now.

She pointed. "There's smoke. His flare's still burning, but it's on the ground."

"He could be hurt," Molly said. "And if we're going to find him, it has to be before that flare goes out."

"We're really going to walk through the jungle at night?" Oliver asked. "With whatever made that *noise* out there?"

Everyone looked at Molly.

"We don't have a choice," she said.

Anna shrugged. "Better keep your sword handy, Yoshi, just in case."

Marching through the jungle at night was unpleasant. Blue glowflies filled the air, branches scratched and tripped, and every scurrying noise in the undergrowth sounded like tanglevine.

On top of which, there was a giant, sharp-clawed creature somewhere out here.

Anna found herself in the lead, using her survival knife to hack a path through the vines. Javi came behind her, holding his water bottle full of glowflies. The cluster of bugs was almost as bright as a flashlight, which saved on batteries. But they also made everyone look like zombies in their pale blue light.

Anna wondered for the hundredth time what the purpose of the bugs' glowing was. Earth insects mostly used bioluminescence for attracting mates. Of course, some jellyfish glowed as a warning—*You don't want to eat me, dude. I'm a jellyfish.*

Were the glowflies poisonous?

Not that Anna was hungry enough to eat bugs. Not yet, anyway.

At least the storm hadn't arrived yet. The cold wind had died down, leaving the jungle silent except for the buzz of insects and the slither of who-knew-what underfoot. But Anna still felt a dampness in the air, like rain coming.

A soft murmur of whispers came from the darkness just ahead. Akiko and Kira had come along, because Molly hadn't wanted to leave them alone. The two girls were so adept at crawling through vines and branches that they didn't bother keeping to Anna's path. She wondered if they'd been secretly exploring the jungle on their own.

She realized they weren't speaking Japanese. The whispers sounded more like French. Right—they'd been flying to Japan from a fancy school in Switzerland.

Were they just practicing their French? Or hiding what they were saying from Yoshi?

The mournful cry came again in the distance, and everyone froze. The leaves seemed to shiver with the sound, and Anna felt it in her spine. Some deep, ancestral part of her knew that she wasn't the top of the food chain right now.

When the cry finally faded, it was a moment before anyone spoke.

"That thing is far away," Javi said softly. "Right?"

"Sure." Molly sounded like she wasn't really certain. "Miles from here."

It was probably true, but Anna heard the metal slither of

Yoshi's sword coming free. The sound sent a little thrill through her, and in that moment something became obvious.

"That was a *call*," she said.

Molly came closer in the darkness. "What do you mean?"

"When an animal makes a noise, it's always for a reason." Anna listened again to the jungle—nothing but the buzz of insects. "A warning, or saying where food is. Or mating."

Javi stared at her, his face lit blue. "You mean, it's talking to another creature like it?"

"So there's *two* of them?" Oliver said.

Anna shrugged. "Nothing answered. But yeah, maybe it's trying to find a friend."

"Better than it trying to find dinner," Molly said.

Anna nodded, and she found herself annoyed again that Caleb had taken the gravity device. They wouldn't have to worry so much about predators if they could fly.

But she didn't say that out loud. Better to say something reassuring.

"Any creature with a call that loud has to be widely dispersed. In other words, there aren't too many of them in this jungle."

"I'm okay with that," Oliver said.

Anna smiled, and didn't add that the scariest predators were often the loneliest. The more they ate, the more territory they needed to themselves.

"Hey, did you feel that?" Javi asked.

Anna had—a familiar flutter in her stomach.

"Like low gravity starting up," she said.

Javi held up his glowing blue bottle. "We must be close. I smell smoke from the flare."

"But the low-G feeling isn't steady. Like the device is fritzing," Molly said. "Maybe you were right about it running out of batteries, Javi."

Anna felt the flutter again, mixed with an awful certainty that the device was broken—she would never fly again.

"Listen," Yoshi whispered.

A silent moment later, Anna heard it. A groan coming from up ahead.

It was a deep, growly, liquid sound, like a lone shredder bird out there in the dark, complaining. It sent another shiver down her spine.

"Could that be . . ." Javi's voice faded.

Anna shook her head. It hadn't sounded human.

"Let's check it out," Molly whispered.

Naifu, came a soft voice from the darkness. Kira emerged from shadow, holding out a hand expectantly.

Anna handed her the knife.

The girl plunged ahead, slashing the vines with near silent efficiency, and the rest of them followed. A moment later they stood at a strange, dark border in the trees.

"Omoshiroi," Kira said.

"Yeah," Anna whispered. "Pretty interesting."

It was as if a line had been drawn through the jungle, a gently curving boundary. Beyond it, no glowflies hovered in the air—a deeper night ruled there. Where the soft light from Javi's bottle touched, the trees seemed gnarled and bent.

"I saw this dark area from back at the bonfire," Anna said. "This is where he went down!"

Another ripple of low gravity went through the air, and the groaning came again.

This time it sounded almost human.

"I'll go first," Javi said. Holding his bottle of glowflies high, he took a step forward.

The instant he crossed the boundary of darkness, a grunt came from his lips. He staggered, dropping to one knee and losing hold of the bottle. It seemed to shoot from his hands to the ground.

"Javi!" Molly followed, reaching out for him. She stumbled as well, but grasped one of the stumpy trees and kept her feet.

Anna started forward, but something held her back.

It was Kira, who had grabbed her belt.

The girl reached her arm out, holding the knife just across the boundary of darkness. Its tip quivered for a moment, until she let it slip from her grasp. It shot from her hand, straight down to *thunk* in the bare dirt.

"Abunai," Kira said softly.

Anna frowned. "I'm going to go with . . . dangerous?"

"Indeed," Yoshi said, standing well back from the darkness. "You okay in there, Javi?"

"I think so." Javi tried to stand but grimaced and sank to his hands and knees. "The gravity in here . . ."

"It's turned *up*," Molly panted, still clinging to the branch.

Anna stared down at the glowflies inside Javi's bottle.

They skittered along the bottom, suddenly too heavy to regain the air. As she watched, they went dark one by one.

"Caleb," she murmured. What if he'd changed the settings on device from light to heavy—*in midair*?

"Go find him!" Molly said. "We'll crawl out!"

"I'll stay here and help!" Oliver said.

Kira pointed to the right, indicating they should try to go around. Together, she, Anna, and Yoshi skirted the border of the darkness.

As they moved, Anna gave the stunted trees a closer look. The fronds were a familiar shape. Of course! This species was everywhere in the jungle, but this area of trees had grown up crushed beneath their own weight. Which meant that whatever was causing this gravity distortion field had been here a *long* time.

Was this heavy gravity *natural*?

In front of her, Kira came to a stop. The growl came again, close by.

"Caleb?" Anna called softly.

Gravity flickered, and words emerged from the darkness.

"Help me."

23

Javi

I t was like being covered in lead.

Javi's aunt Sofia was a cop, and once he'd tried on her bulletproof vest. The Kevlar had felt this heavy, except that here in the high-G zone the weight seemed to be wrapped around his entire body. Every breath struggled into his lungs, as if the air had turned thick and soupy.

But Javi could still crawl, and he made his way to the edge of the darkness, where Akiko and Oliver waited to help. Together, they dragged him out of the gravity distortion field.

Molly came staggering after, collapsing beside him in the undergrowth.

"What's your guess?" she panted. "Double?"

Javi coughed. "At least. How did you keep standing?"

"Five years of ballet," she said. "Gotta thank Mom for that."

"I'll remind you to," Javi said.

Molly had to be worried about her mother, all alone at home. The crash would be on the news by now, of course. Javi closed his eyes, trying not to think about his own family watching TV and worrying.

Instead, he let himself appreciate the merciful normal gravity. He felt like he'd spent a week on Jupiter, and now was finally back on Earth.

But this wasn't Earth. The laws of physics were broken here.

As Javi sat up, another dizzying wave of low G rippled through the air.

"You guys should come," Oliver said. "I think they found Caleb."

Caleb had fallen at the edge of the distortion field.

Of course it was at the edge, Javi realized. The poor guy wouldn't have flown very far in double G. The only thing that had kept him from being squashed outright was the gravity device he'd been carrying. Even now it seemed to be fighting against this heaviness, sending out pulses of low G that grew stronger as Oliver led them closer to where Caleb lay.

As did the awful sound of the guy's breathing.

"I saw . . . something," Caleb was saying.

"Drink this first." Anna was beside him inside the field, bracing her water bottle with both hands. Yoshi was next to her, sitting cross-legged, the strained expression on his face the only sign that he was in double G.

Javi watched as Caleb swallowed, then coughed. It sounded like his lungs were full of tomato sauce.

"In the sky," he managed a moment later.

"That doesn't matter!" Molly cried. "We need to figure out how to get you out of there!"

"We could slide him," Oliver said. "Time it with the flutters of low gravity."

Molly shook her head. "That could hurt him even more."

Anna was staring at the device that lay beside him. "Maybe we can find a higher setting. Something that counteracts the heaviness."

Javi didn't say anything. The way Caleb lay there, his back twisted against the gnarled root of a tree . . . it didn't look good. Maybe if they had a team of paramedics and an ambulance full of medical equipment—double-G Jaws of Life?—something could be done.

But out here in a jungle, with nothing but a survival knife, a first-aid kit, and some water bottles?

Javi glanced at Kira. She shook her head and put her arm around Akiko, who had started to cry.

An awful certainty was creeping into Javi. Caleb wasn't going to make it.

"Stupid . . . kids," the guy croaked. "Listen."

"What is it?" Javi asked softly.

"The moons. They're wrong."

Molly looked up at Javi pleadingly.

"We know," Javi said gently. "We aren't on Earth anymore. But you need to—"

"No." Caleb coughed again, but managed to go on. "The phases are wrong. They're fake."

Javi pictured the moons—two orbs, the red one a little larger. Both of them cratered just like the familiar pale moon back on Earth.

"And the stars," Caleb barely managed.

"You can give us an astronomy report later!" Molly cried.

At those words, a harsh smile formed on Caleb's lips. Another ripple of light gravity passed through the fronds around them, and he managed to slurp a quick breath.

"Urss . . ." he said.

Nobody answered, waiting for more.

But a moment later, Caleb closed his eyes.

"Caleb?" Anna asked. She leaned closer, her neck muscles straining against the gravity.

Nothing. Not even the rattle of his breath.

"Caleb!" Molly cried. When there was no answer, she turned to the others. "We need to get him out of there. Now!"

"Molly," Anna said. "He's not breathing."

Molly stared at her. "What do you mean?"

Anna's face went blank. "He's not breathing because he's dead."

Javi turned away. He couldn't look at Caleb, or at Anna's expression. And most of all he couldn't look at Molly. Her mind was still working, still trying to solve this problem.

But there was nothing to solve.

He didn't know where to look, so Javi watched as a glowfly buzzed past. It drifted into the darkness of the high-G zone, was captured instantly, and fell to the ground.

It was a while before anyone spoke again.

"We should get back to the bonfire," Anna said. "It's getting colder."

"And just leave him?" Molly asked.

Nobody had an answer. The thought of going into the heavy-gravity field again made Javi's stomach churn.

Anna shrugged. "Nature doesn't need help burying the dead."

There was that word again. *Dead.*

People wound up dead in a place like this. That was how nature wanted it—every animal and plant one misstep away from becoming part of the food web. Javi could feel it all around him, the patient hunger of the jungle.

Molly looked like she was about to argue, to say they should have another funeral or even bury him. But then the rain started—a clattering sound, high in the leaves.

It built steadily, but Javi couldn't feel any drops. The thick jungle canopy was protecting them for now. He let the rumble of the rain numb his mind.

"Okay." Molly sounded relieved that a fresh problem had come up. "I guess we need to find shelter."

"Not this close to him," Javi said gently. None of them would sleep.

Molly led them away from the distortion field, to a spot where the jungle canopy was so thick overhead that there was no glimpse of sky. The rain was finally starting to trickle down through the leaves, forming cold, squishy puddles underfoot.

Molly and Anna bent a few of the lower branches closer together and bound them with bungee cords into a makeshift shelter. Everyone huddled together on the roots of the tree, which bulged up high enough to stay dry. The undergrowth here was sparse, which gave the tanglevine less cover to sneak around underfoot.

But tanglevine wasn't the big worry, of course. There was still that foghorn beast out there in the distance, or maybe nearby, its footsteps drowned out by the rain.

Yoshi said he would stand watch and wake one of the others in a few hours. He sat cross-legged at the edge of the roots, facing the trees.

The downpour built until it was too loud to talk. Soon the glowflies had retreated to wherever insects went when it rained, and darkness overtook the jungle.

As she refilled her water bottles from a dripping branch, Molly leaned close to Javi's ear. "It was my idea, him going up to check the stars."

Javi had been waiting for this. "That doesn't make it your fault."

"He'd never even used the device before."

"Yeah, but we didn't know about these . . ." Gravity sinks? Thundersucks? Javi didn't feel like coming up with a name just now. He could still feel the awful weight in his bones, like he'd never crawled out of the high-G zone.

Like the darkness itself had grown heavy.

"I pushed him," Molly said. "He didn't even *want* to jump."

"It was just bad luck."

Molly shook her head. "You can't say that."

"That's what it was."

"But that's even *worse* than it being my fault!"

Javi stared at her. "Why?"

"Because if I made a mistake, no matter how bad, we can learn from it." Molly closed her eyes, her breaths coming short and sharp. "But if something like that can just *happen* here, then we're all . . ."

She didn't finish, but Javi didn't want her to.

"Listen," he said. "We're going to get out of here."

Molly just shook her head, like it was all too much.

"*You're* going to get us out of here," Javi persisted. "You're going to get us home!"

"From an alien world?"

"Caleb said the moons were fake. We're back to not knowing anything about where we are."

"That's not useful! At least an alien planet is a workable theory. Otherwise everything we've seen is just . . . crazy."

Javi shrugged. "Sometimes stuff is crazy."

"How can you deal with nothing making sense?"

He laughed softly. "Have you *met* my family?"

"Your family are the sanest people I know," she said.

Javi gave her a sidelong look, but didn't argue. Molly looked like she was about to cry. And it wasn't fair, arguing about whose family was crazier.

In a funny way, Molly and her mom were the same. Neither of them had ever gotten over how a random disease had just appeared out of nowhere to take Molly's father away. The only difference was, the experience had made Molly a lot more rational—needing to know the whys of everything—and her mother a lot less.

"Caleb's gone, but he helped us," Javi said. "We know that those moons are fake. That has to *mean* something."

"Right," Molly murmured, curling up. "You're right. We'll figure it out."

He watched her close her eyes. Almost by accident, he'd said the right thing—that Caleb had at least given them a clue, a promise that this strange new world could be understood.

But what if that wasn't true?

Javi stared out into the formless dark. There were monsters out there.

He listened to the rain until he managed to fall asleep.

24

Yoshi

he sound was different.

Yoshi shot awake, his hand on his sword hilt. Was it the huge, mournful creature, here in their camp?

Then he realized—the only change was that the rain had stopped. The roar had been replaced by the drip of water through leaves.

He'd fallen asleep on watch. Unforgivable.

He took a slow breath, easing himself upright. Kira was curled up next to him, and she stirred a little. It was still dark, but the glowflies were out again, casting a blue pall over everything.

The others were all asleep, draped like kittens on the roots of the sheltering tree. Anna cradled the gravity device in her arms.

Yoshi stared at it. He could just take the device now and explore all he wanted.

Of course, that would leave the others with a long, dangerous march home. He couldn't do that, especially after what had happened last night.

But Caleb's death only made Yoshi's need to explore greater.

Caleb had said that the moons were fake. Which could mean that the stars were fake, too. What if everything they'd seen had been *designed*?

Yoshi had to know. He reached out and touched the device.

Beside him, Kira opened her eyes. He pulled his hand back.

"You don't have to steal it," she whispered. "There's another one."

He stared at her. "What do you mean?"

Kira pointed back at where they'd left Caleb's body.

"The area of darkness, of heaviness—what if a machine is making it that way?" She gestured at the device in Anna's arms. "A machine like that one."

Yoshi thought for a moment. The high-gravity zone was circular, like the field generated by the device.

But he shrugged. "I don't need something to make me heavier. I need to fly."

"All those symbols," Kira whispered. "Maybe the machine in there is exactly the same, just on a different setting."

Yoshi frowned, remembering the stands of taller trees reaching into the sky. Those areas were also perfect circles, and the same size as the high-gravity zone.

What if they were also caused by devices? If the gravity was set low, the trees would grow taller, wouldn't they?

"But the device was in the plane's cargo," he said. "Why would there be more in this jungle?"

She smiled. "Maybe it wasn't in the cargo. We found it mixed in with the wreckage, but what if it was *already here*? The crash could have dug it up."

Yoshi nodded, but as he stared at the dark circle in the distance, he remembered its awful weight settling over him. The thought of crawling into that heaviness again made his heart sink.

Still, another device would be worth it. "I suppose we could look."

"It's probably buried. It's been here long enough to make those trees grow funny." Kira closed her eyes, drawing shapes in the air with her hand. "But I can help you dig at the exact center of the circle. *If* you promise to take me with you."

He stared at her. "You want to go to the waterfall?"

"Beyond. You're not the only one who wants to know what's going on."

Yoshi sighed. Chances were there wouldn't be any buried device, and he wouldn't have to keep this promise.

"Okay," he said. "Find me a way to fly, and you can come along."

Moving silently in the dark, Kira snuck two flares from Molly's backpack, then led Yoshi through the muddy jungle back to the dark circle of trees.

At the edge, she lit one of the flares and stuck it into a

branch at head level. Yoshi looked back toward their sleeping friends, wondering if he should have woken one of them to keep watch.

Kira followed his gaze and said, "We heard that foghorn thing from miles away. We should be able to hear it from over here."

Yoshi frowned. "Let's make this quick."

Kira led him around the circle to the other side, going the long way to avoid Caleb's body. As she walked, she peered back at the flare just visible through the stunted trees.

Finally, she let out a satisfied grunt. "We're exactly opposite where we started."

"How can you tell?"

She lit the other flare and lodged it in a tree branch. "I just can."

Yoshi frowned. Kira's drawings were always uncannily accurate, and he'd seen her draw a perfect circle freehand. But seeing that two flares, sixty feet apart around a circle, were exactly opposite?

"Spatial reasoning," she added. "It's on all the IQ tests."

"I've never taken one."

"Lucky you," she said.

Yoshi didn't know how to take that. "How am I supposed to tell when I'm halfway between the flares?"

Kira thought for a moment, then sighed. "*You* probably can't. Guess I have to go in, too."

They went on hands and knees, slowly.

The weight felt like an evil twin draped across his back, and Yoshi was careful not to set his knees on the hard, gnarly roots of the trees. The ground, at least, was covered with a soft layer of leaves stripped by the downpour.

Yoshi supposed that even raindrops were heavier in here.

Something gave way beneath his knee with a wet *crunch*, and he paused to brush aside the leaves.

The skeleton of a bird. He wondered how many flew through here accidentally and were captured and crushed.

Like Caleb had been.

Or the airplane itself. Did this heavy zone lie along its flight path?

Yoshi shook the thought away and kept crawling. The plane had been split open from the top endless minutes prior to the crash, long before it could have run into this gravity field.

When the flares looked about the same distance apart, he asked, "Here?"

"A little farther." Kira crawled past him. The extra weight hardly seemed to bother her. Both she and Akiko were short and lithe. Maybe they were suited to high gravity, like the trees around him.

The wind picked up again, and a sprinkling came from the sky. The drops felt hard and cold, and Yoshi was glad he'd left his sword back with the others. He was less happy that he'd wrapped his jacket around it, leaving him wearing nothing but a T-shirt.

"This is the center," Kira finally said.

"Nothing's here," Yoshi sighed.

"I told you, these trees *grew* in this gravity. The device is bound to be under some dirt by now."

"Very *heavy* dirt," Yoshi said.

"That's why I brought this." She pulled out the survival knife.

Yoshi took it and started to dig. With the dirt packed together by double gravity, it was like cutting through clay. When he came across earthworms, they were as tough as metal cables, as if they belonged here in this hard-packed dirt.

He remembered the slide-whistle birds flying expertly in low G. Were all these creatures designed for variable gravity? Or had they *evolved* here?

The cold rain was growing harder. Kira hunkered beneath a nearby tree, trying to stay dry. But getting wet wasn't the worst part—as the rain grew heavier, the drops were beginning to hurt, like cold marbles plunking down on his head.

"Yoshi?" Kira called. "Maybe we should come back later."

He looked up from his digging. She was peering at the sky, her fingers protecting her eyes from the rain.

"Are you kidding?" he asked.

"What if it starts to hail?"

At that moment, a particularly nasty raindrop thwacked Yoshi in the middle of his head. But it trickled, cold and massive, down the back of his neck.

Just heavy rain. "It doesn't hail in jungles."

"You don't know that," she said. "And this isn't a normal jungle!"

"Then I should stop talking and dig!"

He scooped away the water that had collected in the hole and scraped at the packed wet dirt with the knife. His fingers were growing numb, and the knife slipped once, almost cutting him.

Yoshi wondered if you bled faster in double gravity.

The cold, along with the awful weight of everything, was sapping his strength. Breathing was getting harder.

He thought of lying down, just for a moment, to give his muscles a rest. But what if he never regained his strength, and the heavy, freezing water rose above his nose and mouth? Yoshi didn't want to drown in three inches of water.

Correction: He didn't want to drown at *all*.

He plunged the knife in again, and something hard turned the blade. A stone?

Yoshi kept scraping until a curved smoothness emerged from the mud.

"Got it!" he said, pulling at the device with numb fingers.

"Yoshi."

He looked up. Kira was pointing—

Hailstones were bouncing from the ground around them. One smacked his shoulder, as hard as a rock from a slingshot.

"Told you," she said. "What do we do?"

"We turn the gravity down," he said, clawing at the mud.

Another hailstone struck him—like the slap of a wet towel on the back of his neck. Then one struck his hand, pain ringing through his frozen-limbed numbness.

Gradually the device came free—the hard rain was actually helping clear the dirt away. He saw two symbols glowing in the dark, one of them different from the symbols that Anna used for low G.

He'd seen her set the device many times. All you did was press hard on both of the low-G symbols at once . . .

They clicked, then glowed, and the crushing weight lifted from Yoshi. He felt himself drifting into the air.

All at once the rain seemed like a light drizzle, and the branches around him sprang out into new, fuller shapes, as if loads of heavy fruit had dropped from them. The battering hailstones eased, suddenly more like snowflakes than rocks.

Yoshi closed his eyes, breathing deep for the first time since he'd crawled into the dark circle.

A moment later, Kira's voice came from next to him.

"Are you okay?"

"Nothing that a warm fire won't fix," he said.

"Are you going to keep your promise, Yoshi-chan? And let me come along?"

He opened his eyes. "I may be a half, but I always keep my promises."

"Don't be broody," Kira said, then smiled. "They call people like you *halves*, but you've got your Japanese part, and another part as well. So maybe you're really two-in-one. A pair—like me and my sister."

Yoshi sighed and leaned back, letting the rain fall on his face, as soft as feathers.

"I just want to be myself."

25

Molly

I t still feels weird that we just left him out there," Molly said.

Javi didn't answer—he was busy stoking the fire. Everyone had changed into dry clothes when they got back to the airplane that morning, but they were still shivering from the cold night in the rain. Team Killbot all wore scavenged clothes now, the wrong sizes and colors and styles, like they were pretending to be other people.

People who were dead.

"The jungle can handle it," Anna said. She rolled up the too-long sleeves of her shirt, a blank expression on her face.

Molly wasn't in the mood for a biology lesson. The problem with the jungle was, it didn't care about death. And Caleb's death had to mean something, or it would be too awful for any of them to bear.

"But we should say some words, like we did for Mr. Keating. We owe Caleb that much."

Javi stopped blowing on the base of the fire and looked up at her. "He went up to figure out where we are, to help us get home. Succeeding at *that* is what we owe him."

"What was the last thing he said?" Molly asked. "*Urss?* Maybe he was trying to say *Earth.*"

"No," Javi said gently. "It was just *hurts.*"

Anna pointed. "If we want to know what he said, then Yoshi has the right idea."

They all looked up. Yoshi and Kira were using the forward inflatable slide to practice flying with the device they'd found, bouncing off the bright yellow plastic. Akiko watched from below, laughing like this was some kind of theme park.

Alien World. Fun for the whole family.

"I wish they wouldn't make so much noise," Anna said. "That foghorn thing is still out there, and it could be listening."

"Another reason not to go exploring," Molly said.

"But somebody *has* to check out what's past the waterfall," Javi said. "If those really were radio transmissions, it could be a scientific station!"

"Or maybe not," Molly said. No one else had gotten anything but static on the radios. Yoshi's ten seconds of beeping didn't seem like much to go on.

"There have to be people here somewhere," Anna said. "This place isn't natural."

Molly stared into the fire, which hissed with rain-wet

wood. Part of her brain didn't want to deal with theories and conjectures—she just wanted to grieve for Caleb. But another part of her wouldn't stop puzzling it all out.

"What do you mean?" she asked.

"The animals are adapted to the weird physics," Anna said. "The slide-whistle birds know how to fly in low G. And the shredder birds come looking for prey when they sense it. It's like the creatures here evolved alongside this technology."

Javi stared at her. "But how long does it take birds to evolve a new way of flying?"

"Thousands of years?" Anna said. "Millions? So either this technology is very, very old, or everything in this jungle is artificial."

Javi tossed a stick into the fire. "Like, genetically engineered to mess with our minds?"

"No. But engineered for *something*. Which means there are *engineers* somewhere. We just have to find them, and beyond the waterfall is the obvious place to look."

Molly looked out at the jungle. Had the two of them forgotten that someone had *died* out there last night?

She heard the trees creaking in the wind. Or maybe it was just her imagination and the crackle of the fire.

Anna was still watching Kira and Yoshi, who were high in the air, yelling at each other in Japanese.

"You want to go with them, don't you?" Molly asked.

Anna nodded. "We need to know more about this place."

"But every time we leave camp, something tries to kill us! The tanglevine. The shredder birds. And Caleb got killed by what? Gravity. *A law of nature.* And somewhere out there is whatever was making that—"

The foghorn cry came again.

This time it was loud, so close that the small hairs on Molly's neck stood up straight. And it didn't sound mournful . . .

It sounded angry.

"Molly!" Javi hissed, staring straight past her.

"Uh-oh." Anna slowly knelt to pick up the gravity device at her feet.

Molly turned and saw the creature.

It stood on two wrinkled legs, a large flightless bird about halfway between them and the airplane. Its neck stretched into the sky, taller than an ostrich—maybe twelve feet high. Iridescent green feathers stood out from its body, like it was an angry cat with puffed-up fur.

Its head was the strangest thing Molly had ever seen. It seemed to be all beak, like one big razor-sharp scissor made of bone, interrupted only by a pair of beady red eyes.

She imagined the creature scraping that beak against a tree, leaving gouges in the bark, the edges growing sharper and sharper . . .

A cry came from Kira, in the middle of a bounce: *"Abunai!"*

The bird cocked its head, focusing one eye on her and Yoshi as they drifted down toward a petrified Akiko.

"Yep," Anna said. "Dangerous."

"Where's Oliver?" Molly whispered.

Javi pointed. "In the plane."

Kira and Yoshi landed next to Akiko and grabbed her hand, and together they jumped back toward the aircraft.

The giant bird ruffled its feathers and took a step toward them. Its powerful legs bent beneath it . . .

Molly's mind spun. What if this bird was also adapted to low gravity? Yoshi's sword would be useless in midair.

"Hey, bird!" Molly yelled, and the creature hesitated, pointing a baleful red eye at her.

She whirled toward the fire and grabbed the biggest burning stick she could see. Smoke and sparks spilled from the fire as she dragged it out. "Give me low G, *now*!"

"You got it," Anna said, pressing buttons.

Weightlessness fluttered through Molly as she flung the burning stick. It spun through the air until it hit the edge of the gravity field. Its flight bent down then, but momentum still carried it onward. It struck the ground and rolled, smoking and sparking, almost to the giant bird's clawed feet.

The bird hopped back from the stick, its talons leaving deep scrapes in the wet ground.

"Ready for heavy," Anna said, and normal weight settled over them.

The bird stretched its neck forward and let out a long *hiss* at Molly, a long green tongue flickering from its maw.

"I think you made it mad," Anna said.

Molly couldn't argue with that. The bird was advancing now, its stubby wings puffed out even more, making it seem bigger, scarier. The feathers looked barbed at the end, like a shiny green mass of fishhooks coming straight at her.

She reached for another flaming stick.

"Please be afraid of fire," she whispered.

Javi had lunged for the survival pack and was rifling around inside. He pulled out the survival knife and held it up before himself.

Those inches of steel looked puny in comparison to the charging bird. The heavy thump of its strides traveled through the ground and shook the soles of Molly's feet.

This is how the jungle works, she realized. You stumbled around, having theories and solving problems, until something bigger than you came along.

Then you got eaten.

From twenty yards away, the bird took a mighty bound, its huge legs propelling it into the air. It arced toward Molly, a huge missile of razor beak and hooked feathers and muscle.

She held the burning stick in front of her . . .

A crushing weight descended on Molly, and the charging bird tumbled to the ground. It hit hard, rolling toward her in a cloud of dust and thrashing talons.

She tried to leap aside, but in the double gravity her feet felt dipped in concrete. She only managed a single step before the angry mass of claws and feathers swept past her. Pain blossomed across her shoulder.

The bird rolled into the fire, scattering smoke and sparks. It began to shriek like a pipe organ, a high-pitched version of its foghorn cry.

Then the heaviness lifted, straight from double gravity to almost weightless, and everything around Molly seemed to fly apart. Flaming wood exploded from the fire, along with clouds of dust, burned feathers, and scavenged clothing. The bird launched itself shrieking into the air, and Molly lofted backward in an aerial somersault. She caught a glimpse of Javi floating away, knife flailing blindly in the smoke.

"Ready for normal!" Anna's voice came from the chaos.

Molly hit the ground as gravity settled onto her, landing with an *oof*. Smoking firewood was scattered everywhere, along with feathers and survival gear.

"Everyone okay?" Anna asked, her arms cradling the gravity device.

"I think so?" Javi was nearby, his eyes wide and searching. "But where's the bird?"

Molly squinted through the smoke and dust—

The creature rose up from a huddle at the edge of the forest and cast an angry glare at them through its red eyes. It looked singed and ruffled, and it limped as it turned to face them.

But it still looked ready to fight.

Molly stood carefully. "You ready to hit that double gravity again?"

Anna nodded, but then another flutter of lightness went through Molly—and Yoshi went drifting past overhead. He landed between the scattered campfire and the wounded giant bird and drew his sword with a flourish, metal glittering in the sun.

The bird glowered at him a moment and let out the long, mournful foghorn blast of its cry. Then it turned and limped into the jungle, thrashing at the palm fronds with its claws.

A moment later it was gone.

Molly managed a smile, but then a wave of dizziness came over her.

She looked down at her right shoulder. Her sleeve was in ribbons, and a single deep cut oozed blood. Some kind of green liquid surrounded the wound. It was shiny, pulsing in the sunlight.

"That's weird," she said.

Anna came closer and stared. "Does it hurt?"

Molly shook her head. All of a sudden, *nothing* hurt. Not the cut or her bruises or her smoke-filled lungs. Suddenly, everything was soft and hazy, and she was so tired that she could barely keep her eyes open . . .

By the time she tumbled forward into the grass, Molly felt nothing at all.

The next morning at dawn they said good-bye at the stream. Yoshi's plan was to follow it back to the waterfall, then go beyond. Not a terrible plan, Molly thought. But the *beyond* part sounded fuzzy.

Of course, *everything* sounded fuzzy today.

The cut on her shoulder still glowed iridescent green, as if the bird had left the glimmer of its plumage in her. No matter how much she washed it, the green didn't go away.

But it didn't hurt, not at all. In a way, the mysterious numbness was worse than pain would've been.

"It's all here," Anna said. She'd filled two backpacks with gear: knives, flashlights, fire starters, signal mirrors, and a first-aid kit. She, Yoshi, and Kira were taking the remaining flares and packaged food, which wouldn't be needed at camp anymore.

The night before, Akiko had reluctantly agreed to lure another slide-whistle bird to its doom. Yoshi had missed with his sword, but Javi had caught the bird in a cargo webbing net. Javi himself had narrowly escaped accidental death by sword—bad planning on everyone's part—but the bird had roasted up wonderfully with *omoshiroi*-berries.

Now that it was time to part, Akiko was crying and hugging Kira. Yoshi looked embarrassed, and Anna had the same blank stare she'd worn since Caleb's death.

Not the most promising start to the trip, Molly thought. The cold wind hadn't returned last night, and the glowflies were thicker than usual in the dawn light. The jungle buzzed like a broken neon light.

"We'll be back in three days," Anna said, and kissed Molly lightly on the cheek. "We'll bring help. People who know how to fix that infection . . . or whatever it is."

Molly smiled, wondering if Anna was really that confident, or if this was one of her white lies. Molly decided to lie herself.

"I know you'll be back. You've only got three days' worth of food, after all."

"We should get started, then." Yoshi shouldered his backpack, looking impatient to leave Akiko's tears behind.

Anna picked up the new gravity device. "Take care of Oliver. And watch out for wounded killer birds."

"Don't worry about us," Molly said as the sudden pulse of low G made her heart flutter. Then Anna, Kira, and Yoshi leaped gently up to the treetops, and a moment later they were gone.

Normal gravity descended, and for a moment no one said anything.

Molly broke the silence. "Maybe we all should have gone. Just to keep everyone together."

"You aren't going anywhere until that wound heals," Oliver said.

"It doesn't even hurt."

Suddenly, Molly felt meek and useless for staying here instead of exploring. But the feeling only lasted until another wave of dizziness went through her, about the hundredth since the giant bird had left its poison in her blood.

What was happening inside her?

And how much longer did she have to wait to find out?

26

Anna

I t took most of the day to reach the waterfall.

Kira was a strong jumper, but she and Yoshi couldn't seem to get in sync. When their timing was wrong, the three of them spun in lazy circles, leaving Anna feeling like she'd swallowed a pukeberry. It didn't help that Kira and Yoshi kept arguing with each other in Japanese, presumably about whose fault it was.

When the roar of the waterfall finally grew near, Anna was almost happy to worry about tanglevine instead of motion sickness.

They alighted on the big rock that overlooked the falls. Once they'd untied themselves, Yoshi stood staring at the undergrowth, ready to draw his sword.

"Refill the water bottles," he said. "But be careful."

Anna rolled her eyes.

"I'm taking a bath," she said, then mimed washing herself for Kira.

Kira nodded and pulled off her jacket.

"It's pretty cold," Yoshi warned.

"Cold sounds great." Anna was hot and sweaty, and she wanted to wash away the thought that Molly was probably getting sicker every minute. "Anyway, jumping in is the easiest way to fill the bottles without getting near the undergrowth."

"If the vine attacks, I'll kill it," Yoshi said. "Then we can use it as climbing rope."

She stared at him. "You want to use me as bait?"

"I didn't mean it like that." He looked away. "It's just that tanglevine could be useful."

Anna almost smiled. In a way, Yoshi was like her— practical about what was necessary to survive, and a little too blunt about saying it out loud.

But she did feel safe with him around. And nothing was more necessary at the moment than a cold bath.

She dropped her jacket and backpack onto the rock but kept the rest of her clothes on. She might not have another chance to wash them on this expedition. Besides, Yoshi was right there.

Anna steeled herself before jumping in, but when she hit the water, the icy reality forced a shriek from her lungs. Kira smirked down at her from the rock, but when she plunged in, she also let out a squeak.

When the two crawled back out, Yoshi looked up from his radio with a grin.

"Told you it was cold."

Anna tried to shrug, but it turned into a shiver.

"Anything?" she asked through chattering teeth.

He looked up into the misty spray of the falls. "Just static. But I swear, I heard something the first time I was here."

Anna sat up and began to squeeze water out of her shirt. "I'm not doubting you."

She didn't have a choice but to believe Yoshi. Finding other people was the only hope for making Molly better. Anna couldn't wipe away the image of the wound, shimmering like a green insect's wings.

As she and Yoshi had crossed the jungle that afternoon, they'd twice heard the cry of the giant bird echoing across the jungle. And both times it had come from back near the crash. Anna just hoped that the others were safe.

Kira was squeezing out her hair. The red color from the *omoshiroi*-berries was partly washed out, but now she was rubbing in some of the blue berries, turning it a faint purple color.

She said something in Japanese, and Yoshi nodded in agreement.

"We should start climbing," he said.

Anna followed his skyward gaze into the mists. There was probably a whole other biome up there, with its own food web, its own edible plants and animals. Its own predators, too, of course.

And hopefully people—or aliens, whoever might have a cure for Molly.

Anna suspected that whatever was up there, it was going to be very *omoshiroi.*

"Okay," she said. "Let's go."

They retied the bungee cords and began to climb. The incline grew steeper and steeper, until it was almost vertical—a wall of stone.

It was like climbing in a dream. The only sound was the roar of rushing water beside them. Thanks to the gravity device, Anna could hold her own weight with one hand—or just a couple of fingers when she wanted to get fancy. The tricky part was hanging on when a strong breeze tried to tug them from the wall of rock. The thought of falling all the way back down, even in low G, made her queasy.

And what if shredder birds attacked? They couldn't turn off the device without falling to their deaths.

It took the first hour for Anna to relax. The birds probably didn't fly this high. Not that she had any real idea about their altitude—the swirling clouds erased everything except her two companions.

"Shouldn't we be able to see by now?" she asked. "I mean, the mist out in the jungle only went a couple of hundred feet up."

Yoshi stopped and hung from one hand, taking a drink of water. "Where does mist come from?"

"Water evaporating from the jungle. But we're way too high for that." Anna looked up. "This mountain must have clouds rolling down it."

Yoshi nodded, then started translating for Kira, and Anna paused for a quick drink. Her fingers were starting to cramp. The wall of stone was so flat—there was no place to rest, not even an outcrop big enough to plant her feet on.

Maybe it really was a wall, a huge one. *But what was it keeping out?*

There was no way to find out except to keep climbing to the top.

By the time the sun started to set, both of Anna's hands were aching. She might not weigh much, but holding on to the rocks was like carrying an egg for hours straight with no place to put it down—one slip and it was broken.

"What if we never find a place to stop?" she asked. "What if this just goes up forever?"

"Don't think about that," Yoshi said. "We keep going until we get to the top."

"Sure," Anna said, but a slow panic was building inside her. She tried to remind herself—even if she lost her grip and pulled the others free, they would only drift back down together like a handful of feathers.

But they'd lose the whole afternoon's climb, and the breeze could carry them miles away from where they'd started. And any rescue for Molly would be another day away.

Just then, a low, familiar moan came from the jungle below.

"Yokaze," Kira said.

Yoshi translated, "The night wind."

"Good name," Anna said, and shivered. It was the same

cold wind that had swept through the jungle two nights before, taking Caleb away to his death.

If the three of them fell now, the night wind might carry them over a double-G zone—they'd all be smashed to jelly. Or they might drift into the roaring waterfall.

Anna just hoped her fingers didn't get too cold to function. The air seemed to be getting colder every minute they climbed.

"We should have brought gloves," she said.

Yoshi managed a shrug. "I told you it would be cold."

Anna sighed—she *had* brought a jacket. But she'd tied it around her waist at the start of the climb, and now there was no way to put it on.

Then she felt it, the *yokaze* ruffling her hair, reaching its cold fingers beneath her shirt. A shiver trembled along her spine.

Then a sudden gust hit, and her right hand slipped free from the rock.

Her left hand was holding one of the scrubby plants that clung to the rocks, and it came loose, too—she found herself drifting away from the wall of stone, grabbing at air.

"Uh, guys," she said. *"Abunai!"*

The cloudy abyss opened up beneath Anna. Even floating in low G, the yawning drop made her stomach flip inside out.

She forced herself to freeze—flailing would only make it harder for the others to hang on. Kira and Yoshi were scrambling to take hold of whatever they could.

The bungee cords slowly stretched, went taut, and then pulled her gently back toward the rocks. Anna reached out for a pair of handholds, her heart pounding in her throat.

"Sorry," she said, clinging gratefully to the rock. "I grabbed the wrong plant."

Yoshi's face looked pale, but he said calmly, "When rock climbing, never trust vegetation."

"Especially here, where it can eat you." Anna tried to laugh at her own joke, but it came out more like a whimper.

"Yoshi!" called Kira, then added more in Japanese.

Anna looked up. The night wind had cleared the mist a little, and a dark shape was forming in the rocks above Kira.

The mouth of a cave.

"Maybe we should rest," Yoshi said.

Anna stared at him. *"Maybe?"*

A minute later they were all inside the cave. The *yokaze* roiled around its mouth, still threatening to pull them back out into the misty air.

"Ready for heavy?" Anna said.

The other two nodded, and she switched the device off.

Normal gravity tumbled down like a sack of doorknobs. Anna dropped to her knees on the stone. After hours of climbing in low G, the muscles in her hands were burning, but the rest of her felt rubbery and weak. And hungry.

"Ow," Kira said, rubbing her hands.

"No kidding." Anna's cold, sore fingers struggled to unzip her backpack. She could smell the food bars through their wrapping and was already appalled that they'd only rationed two for each meal.

She pulled one out and tore it open, wolfed it down, then took a long and welcome drink of water. Kira was ripping open packets as well, and somehow the scent of stale airplane pretzels made Anna's mouth water.

Then she noticed how warm it was in the cave and placed her palm flat against the ground.

The stone was warm to the touch.

Kira crunched a pretzel, and the sound echoed back at them from the depths of the cave.

"There's some kind of passage back there," Anna said softly.

Yoshi nodded, but he was listening to his radio. Instead of the usual hiss of static, a soft sound was coming from it.

Beep, beep, beep . . .

A warm rush of relief went through her. It was definitely some kind of transmission, the ordered pulse of civilization. The sound of medicine and food and nothing trying to eat you.

Maybe Molly was going to be okay. Maybe they were all going to get home.

Yoshi listened for a while, then placed it beside him and sat cross-legged, staring out at the mist.

"Aren't you hungry?" Anna asked. "Or do you want to explore the cave first?"

"Let's wait for that. The night wind is clearing the air, and this is higher than we've ever been." He sipped from his water bottle. "Soon, we'll finally be able to see where we are."

Anna looked at Kira, who handed her some pretzels and shrugged.

But Yoshi was right—as the sunset turned the mists to shades of rust and rose, shapes began to form on the dark horizon. The *yokaze* was clearing away the clouds, and the landscape below was coming into focus.

The three of them settled in the cave mouth, staring out, hoping for some sliver of the truth to be revealed.

27

Javi

D on't feel left out, Molly." Javi wiped his lips with a linen napkin from first class. "Those suckers out in the jungle are eating peanuts and stale pretzels, while we feast on roasted slide-whistle bird!"

"Which we also had for lunch," Oliver pointed out. "And breakfast."

Javi stared at him. "Are you dissing the bird?"

"No." Oliver turned to Molly. "But maybe we should try something new. Like those purple berries growing under the left wing."

"You get to eat the first one," Javi muttered.

Slide-whistle bird and *omoshiroi*-berries were like chicken and mashed potatoes—Javi could eat them every day and not get bored.

Or maybe it was just how hungry he was. The four of them

had spent all afternoon turning the aircraft into an anti-giant-bird fort, and by the time dinner was ready he was hungry enough that *everything* tasted good.

It had been worth the effort, though. Up here in first class, the seats were like little rooms built into the cabin floor. They hadn't been torn out from their roots like the flimsy ones back in economy. Once Javi and the others had mopped up last night's rain, hauled out some wreckage, and replaced the missing cushions, the cabin was luxurious again! The ripped-open roof let in the cool night air—just the right amount of nature for Javi. And once Oliver had found the first-class plates and glasses, things had gotten downright civilized.

Maybe it was a little creepy, eating dinner where the missing passengers had sat. But it felt a lot safer than sleeping outside. Javi would take uneasy ghosts over carnivorous vines and giant birds any day.

As a bonus, the first-class galley's storage drawers had contained little bottles of Tabasco, which spiced up the *omoshiroi* sauce perfectly.

As the others finished, Akiko wiped her hands and picked up her flute. Javi wondered what it was like for her, having no one to talk to now that Yoshi and Kira were gone. But Akiko didn't seem to mind. She'd worked happily on the airplane all day and now seemed content to listen to the birds outside and learn their songs.

As Molly cleaned off her fork and knife, she said, "Maybe we should do something useful tonight."

Javi frowned at her. Her face was pale, and though the wound from the bird was covered with a bandage now, it had glowed that strange green the last time Molly had cleaned it.

"We already built a luxury jungle fortress," he said. "Maybe you should rest."

Molly shook her head. "I'm fine."

"No, you're *not*," Oliver said. "You can't just pretend that bird didn't do something weird to you!"

"You mean 'the dreadful duck of doom'?" Molly said with a smile.

Oliver just glared at her, and then at Javi, whose first attempt at a name for the creature had maybe been a little inappropriate.

"Oliver, I'm not going to lie to you," Molly said gently. "I feel weird, but we can't just sit here while the others take all the risks. We should do something to help us find a way home."

When Oliver didn't answer, Javi spoke up. "Like what?"

"We could try some new symbols on the device."

Javi found himself wishing he hadn't asked. Anna, Kira, and Yoshi had taken the new gravity device—the one they'd found at the center of the heavy-gravity zone—on their expedition. But the old one was still here.

"How does that help us get rescued?" Oliver asked.

Molly shrugged. "We don't know yet. But if this machine can mess with the laws of physics, who knows what else it can do?"

Javi wondered if Molly just wanted to distract Oliver, or if she really thought they could find a way home. Or—and this made it *really* hard to argue—maybe she just wanted to go out swinging.

"Let's review," Molly said.

They were all a hundred yards from the plane—close enough to flee to safety if the dreadful duck of doom showed up. Though, frankly, closer would have made Javi happier.

"We know these two symbols turn the gravity to low," she said. "And if you switch to *this* one, it turns the gravity up high instead."

Javi turned on his flashlight for a better look. All the symbols looked like squiggles to him. No handy up or down arrows to help it all make sense.

Which was either bad design . . . or *alien* design.

"So the symbol they have in common means *gravity*," Oliver said.

"Let's not mess with that one," Javi said. "I mean, we don't want to get squished, right? Or reverse gravity and fly up into space!"

"Agreed," Molly said. "But if we use the *low* and *high* symbols, it's sort of like a controlled experiment."

Javi frowned. "So what's safer, low or high?"

"I guess that depends on what the other symbol does," Molly said.

"About which we have no idea," Oliver pointed out. "We

could pick a symbol that means *high intensity pain*. Or low could be, *Hey, device, turn the oxygen down low!*"

Javi stared at Molly. "And you're *sure* this is a good idea?"

"Just one new setting," she said. "It could change everything, like flying did."

It sure changed everything for Caleb, Javi thought. The mournful sound of Akiko's flute wafted on the night breeze, like the song of a ghost. She didn't seem to know any happy tunes.

"Low was safer for gravity," Javi finally said. "Let's start there."

Molly looked at Oliver, who gave her a shrug.

"Low it is," she said, and pressed one of the first two symbols Anna had discovered. Then she turned the inner ring, counting off the others with, "Eeny, meeny, miny . . ."

Javi swallowed, keeping his flashlight trained on the mysterious symbols. It was like drawing straws again, and somehow he *knew* they were going to wind up with pukeberries. Akiko stopped playing her flute, watching intently.

"Get ready for . . . whatever," Molly said, and pressed the chosen button.

Javi waited for some epic change in the laws of nature, but nothing happened for a moment. Then his flashlight flickered.

"Huh," Molly said. "Out of batteries?"

Javi shook the flashlight. "We've hardly used this one since . . ."

He looked closer. The little bulb was glowing in there, barely.

"Um," he said. "I think you just set my flashlight to *low*."

"Okay," Oliver said. "That's not *quite* as cool as messing with gravity. Are you sure it's not just broken?"

"One way to check." Molly switched the device off.

The flashlight flickered back to life, the beam steady and normal again.

"Omoshiroi," Oliver said. "What about the other way? Set it to high."

Molly shrugged. "How bad could it be?"

"Now that you mention it"—Javi set the flashlight down on a rock and stepped away—"it can *always* be bad."

"Okay," Molly said. "Ready for turned-up flashlight?"

"Ready," Oliver said, and Javi just shrugged.

When she activated the device again, the flashlight's bulb flared to life, throwing a blindingly bright beam out into the jungle.

"Omoshiroi des ne," Akiko said.

"Whoa!" Javi touched the flashlight gingerly. It was a little hot, and when he tried to turn it off, the switch did nothing. The buzz of the night was growing louder around them, a swarm of insects roiling into the dazzle of the beam.

"Turn it off, Molly!" Oliver yelped. "We might be signaling that giant bird!"

"Okay." She pressed buttons, and a moment later the light faded.

Javi found himself blinded, blinking away spots and tracers. Akiko muttered to herself in Japanese, rubbing her eyes.

Molly lifted the flashlight from Javi's grip, turned it back on.

"It still works."

A little vibrating noise came from somewhere.

"Was that a *phone*?" Javi asked, still blinking away spots.

Oliver pulled a phone from his pocket. It was glowing, and a charging symbol filled its screen. "Wow. I took photos with this until the battery was completely dead!"

"So we can recharge human tech," Molly said. "Which means we'll always have light. We don't need those stupid glowflies anymore!"

"Don't dis the glowflies," Javi muttered. For one thing, the amped-up flashlight was *way* too strong. His vision still swam with flares.

"Maybe we can use equipment from the plane," Oliver said. "The computers, the air conditioner. And the radios, to talk to each other!"

Javi stared at the device, then at Molly.

"Are you thinking what I'm thinking?" she asked.

He nodded. "That the transmitters on the plane have way more range than those handheld radios? And that maybe we can signal whoever's out there from the comfort of our luxury anti-bird fortress?"

"Yep," Molly said.

Javi smiled. Maybe this *was* better than altering gravity.

He turned and headed for the plane.

Even after all the strange technology and alien wildlife, the jetliner cockpit was still one of the coolest things Javi had ever seen.

The front windows had been torn out by the weird electricity during the crash, but the controls remained—about a thousand gauges and buttons. They took up every square inch of the walls and ceiling. Sweeping his flashlight across them, Javi remembered Molly's trivia question about three hundred miles of wire. He could believe it.

Akiko sat down in the pilot's seat and took the rudder in her hands.

"Do we even know where the radio is?" Oliver asked.

Molly pointed. "There's a headphone jack. The radio could be those switches next to it."

"But there's a lot of other stuff in here," Oliver said. "Maybe start on the low setting."

"Right." Molly held up the device. "Get ready for low tech."

Akiko placed her hands in her lap and nodded.

When Molly pressed the buttons, Javi's flashlight wavered again, and the cockpit went dark except for the tepid glow of its bulb. Nothing glimmered on the blank screens, and none of the dials twitched.

Akiko reached up and took the rudder controls again. She turned them left and right. Javi stuck his head out the empty right window, peering back at the dark wing. It looked just as broken as it had been since the crash.

He pulled his head back in. "Nothing happening."

Oliver thumped a motionless dial. "Maybe the low setting only affects machines that already work."

"Well, then," Molly said. "Get ready for *high* tech."

Javi turned off his flashlight and took a deep breath.

Suddenly, the cockpit came to life. The dials glowed a cheery orange, their needles fluttering. The screens lit up with aircraft outlines and scrolling numbers, and red lights flickered everywhere.

Akiko cried out happily and clapped her hands.

"Whoa," Javi said. "This is an airplane again!"

"It almost feels like it could fly," Molly breathed. "Except for the broken wings."

A small, insistent beep began to play, and they all looked at each other.

"Can anyone find that?" Molly asked. "It might be a signal!"

Akiko pointed at a row of lights between the pilots' chairs. They were blinking red—exactly in time with the beeping.

Then Javi saw the levers just below them—they were pushed halfway up.

"Uh-oh," he said. "I think the pilots left the engines on."

Another bank of lights went red, and more shrieking noises sounded.

The beeps weren't signals, Javi realized. They were *alarms*.

Suddenly, the plane lurched beneath them, all two hundred forty feet of it rocking from side to side.

"Switch it off!" Javi yelled, but Molly had already stabbed at the device's buttons.

The cockpit flickered back into darkness around them. The alarms went mercifully silent.

"Phew," Javi said. His ears rang with the cacophony of a moment before, but he could still hear something—a metal whine coming from outside.

He stuck his head out the window again and switched on the flashlight.

The inner right engine was in motion, the huge jet turbine spinning fast. Its blades were shattered and warped, and they scraped with a chorus of shrieks against the engine housing. Sparks and pieces of loose metal flew in all directions.

As Javi watched, an outline of blue flame went shooting down the wing.

28

Molly

When Javi pulled his head back inside, his face was pale.

"What?" Molly asked, then sniffed the air. "Is that . . ."

"Fire," he croaked, just as the *whuff* of an explosion came through the air, along with a blast of heat.

The airplane rocked beneath Molly's feet, sending her staggering across the cockpit. She grabbed for the copilot's chair to keep her footing, and the device slipped from her hand.

"Everyone out!" she cried. "Head for the slide!"

In a mad scramble, Oliver, Akiko, and Javi pushed their way out of the cockpit door. Molly knelt to retrieve the device, but it was wedged beneath the navigator's seat. She clawed at it, finally managing to yank it free and stumble from the cockpit. Pain bloomed in her bird-bitten right shoulder, and dizziness swept through her as she stood.

The first-class cabin was a jumble of pillows and blankets, askew from the moments the plane had been set rocking. The remains of dinner were strewn on the floor—dishes, plates, salt and pepper packets, tiny bottles of Tabasco.

The scent of a fire filled the air, as oily and sharp as kerosene.

Jet fuel.

"Abunai!" came Akiko's voice, as clear as a bell through the roar.

Molly ran into the next cabin and found the other three at the emergency door. Akiko had her arms spread across the door to keep the others from jumping.

Oliver turned to Molly. "The slide, it's deflating!"

"The engine was throwing off fragments," Javi said. "Must have put a hole in it!"

Molly waited for a moment as her dizziness passed, then said, "We can fly down. Everybody huddle up!"

The four of them crowded together at the door, arms around one another. The whole wing glowed, and a column of smoke was rising in the darkness. The heat pummeled Molly's face like an oven with an open door.

She realized that Javi had a pillowcase under one arm, which bulged with the shapes of silverware and tiny bottles.

"Seriously?" she cried.

"If this plane burns, we might never taste Tabasco again!"

"Whatever. Jump on a count of three—*away* from the wing!" Molly switched the device on, and weightlessness hit. "One, two . . ."

They jumped raggedly and wound up spinning around one another in the air. Their angle was too high, and as they were coming down a breeze caught them.

Not a breeze—the intake of the spinning turbine.

The three of them began to drift toward the burning engine.

"Make us heavy!" Oliver cried.

Molly stared at the ground, thirty feet below. "Too high!"

Javi swung his pillowcase and shouted, "Third law!"

He flung the sack hard, straight up into the air, and Molly felt its gentle push downward. As they neared the burning engine, the heat grew. Javi threw his flashlight skyward, pushing them still lower . . .

At ten feet up, she switched the device off, and they all went crashing down.

A *thud* went through Molly when she hit the ground, and her arm exploded with pain. A fresh wave of dizziness struck her.

She blinked it away. The scorching wind was still building, dragging her toward the fire. The engine whined and sputtered, its spinning turbine pulling air into the engine, which burned fuel, which powered the turbine—the cycle wouldn't stop on its own.

In fact, it was getting stronger! Molly saw Akiko, the smallest of them, skidding across the ground toward the engine.

"Abunai!" Akiko called.

Oliver grabbed her, but then he was being pulled in as well.

Behind them, the pillowcase full of Tabasco fell from the sky and was sucked into the engine. It was vaporized in a flash.

Molly reached through the blistering heat for the device, a few feet away. She stabbed at the buttons—

Double gravity hit, flattening her to the ground. Akiko and Oliver dropped as well, not skidding anymore, but the fire blossomed . . .

The air that fueled it was growing heavier, Molly realized. Denser and more oxygen rich!

Ignoring the crushing weight that made her injured shoulder scream, Molly managed to stab the buttons again, setting the device to low tech.

The weight lifted, and at once the spinning turbine began to sputter. The shriek of metal against metal dropped in pitch as the engine ground to a noisy, ragged halt.

Jet fuel still burned, but it was no longer fed by a roaring wind. She and the others beat a hasty retreat toward the jungle, until the blistering heat finally faded.

They collapsed in the undergrowth, Molly panting, her lungs scorched. The kerosene smell of jet fuel clung to her, and her face and arms still carried the fire's heat.

Her shoulder pulsed with pain.

"Okay," she said when she could talk again. "Playing with settings: bad idea."

"Told you," Oliver said.

Molly stared back at the plane. A skyscraper of smoke now towered above it, disappearing into the mists above. The fire's roar was a gentle rumble almost lost in the buzz of glow-flies around them.

"We only had one dinner in first class," Javi moaned. "And all my Tabasco's gone!"

"I'm sorry for your loss," Molly said. "But it saved us from a fiery death."

"Yeah," Javi said. "But we don't have an anti-bird fortress anymore."

Molly glanced at her wounded shoulder—the bandage had been knocked askew. Out here in the darkness, the wound's green tinge was actually glowing, casting a green pall on the skin around it.

She looked up to find Javi staring at it, too, and tried to smile.

"It doesn't hurt. Much. I'm more worried about that bird."

"At least we've got a fire to scare it away," Oliver said, pointing at the plane.

But a moment later the flames sent a final *whuff* of heat across Molly's skin, and the fire began to sputter and die, its fuel expended.

They were silent then, and Molly felt the jungle's darkness swallow them.

29

Yoshi

T here's something happening out there," Anna said.

Yoshi's eyes sprang open, and he took a sharp breath. Leaning against the warmth of the cave wall, he'd almost dozed off.

But when he saw it, he came fully awake—a flare of light had appeared on the dark horizon.

"Interesting," Kira said, her fingers playing with the new purple streak in her hair.

As Yoshi stared, the light grew brighter. Only a thin layer of mist clung to the jungle now, and the billowing flames tore through it. A tower of smoke rose into the darkness, slicing away a column of stars.

The night wind had cleared the sky an hour ago, revealing that Caleb had been right. The moons were too low in the sky to be real. They looked more like illuminated balloons float-ing a little higher than the level of the cave.

Whether this was Earth or not, someone was messing with them.

From up here, the rolling contours of the jungle were visi-ble. Way off in the distance—another wall of stone stretched across the horizon, covered with streaming waterfalls. Yoshi hoped the morning would show more.

The radio was still beeping, the patterns always changing, but no one had answered his calls.

"Wait a second," Anna said. "Isn't that fire close to—"

The firelight blossomed brighter, tearing away the last veil of mist. For a moment, Yoshi saw a line of scars in the jungle canopy.

The crash site, with the fire at one end of it.

All that jet fuel Molly had worried about, always making them build their bonfires far away from the wings. But the engineers wouldn't have been so careless, would they?

Kira gave Yoshi a questioning look.

"Anna thinks the plane's burning," he said in Japanese. "She might be right."

Kira turned to stare at the distant fire, and her breathing halted for a moment.

"My sister," she said raggedly, and for a second Yoshi thought she was about to have a panic attack. But then Kira reached for her drawing pad, and a moment later her trembling hands had steadied, her pencil a soft whisper in the darkness.

The light flared again, sending another dark billow into the sky. The column of smoke grew taller every moment.

"We have to go back," Anna said.

"No," Yoshi said. "It would take us all night to get back. We have to keep looking for help."

"But they could be hurt," Anna said. She'd always seemed so calm to Yoshi, so strong, but now her voice was breaking.

"Jumping in the darkness is what killed Caleb." Yoshi felt awful for saying it, but it was true.

"You think they're okay?" Kira asked. Her voice suddenly sounded more like Akiko's, gentle and uncertain.

Yoshi needed to be certain for all of them.

"They can take care of themselves," he said in English. "It's our job to explore this cave and see if we can find help. Not in the morning. Now."

Anna took a halting breath, then nodded, her old self again.

Kira closed her drawing pad and started to pack, not needing any translation.

When the scuttling sound came again, Yoshi froze in the darkness.

Something was moving back there in the depths of the cave. He'd heard it almost since the first moment they'd entered the passages that led deeper into the wall of stone.

He reached for his sword and drew a few inches of bright steel.

"Light," he whispered in Japanese.

Kira switched on her flashlight, and a beam shot into the depths of the cave.

Some kind of machine stood there.

It was about the size of a brick and had eight legs, four on each side. Two metal whiskers stuck out of it, waving like antennae in the breeze from the cave mouth.

As if it was tasting the air.

They all froze as it scuttled closer to them, moving in a darting burst of speed, like a metal insect.

Yoshi eased his katana back into its sheath. Striking the metal robot would only nick the blade, and the thing looked small enough to toss against the wall if it came to that. But it didn't look dangerous.

"What is it?" he asked in English.

"How should I know?" Anna asked.

"You're the robot expert."

"*Soccer-playing* robot expert. No idea what *that* thing is for." Emotion flooded her usually calm voice. "Except it means there are people around somewhere. Maybe we *can* find help."

The machine moved again, scurrying closer to Kira. She drew back against the cave wall but kept her flashlight steady on the robot. Its metal whiskers extended . . .

Then coiled around the flashlight and snatched it from her hand!

Kira yelped, scooting backward. She picked up a rock the size of her hand and readied to attack.

"No!" Anna whispered. "We need to follow it back to whoever made it."

Yoshi started to translate, but Kira waved him silent, the rock still ready.

The robot hefted the flashlight, turning it around—as if investigating. More whiskers emerged, waving like stalks of grass.

Then the machine crawled toward Anna. She tensed but didn't move.

It seemed to ignore her, but another of its metal whiskers reached for her backpack . . . and drew out the gravity device. More whiskers extended to wrap around it, touching each of the symbols.

Then the robot began to drag the gravity device away.

Kira looked at Yoshi. "Um, what do we—"

With a *crash*, Anna brought her foot down hard, sending metal parts skittering in all directions across the cave floor.

The robot was still moving, but only barely. A few of its legs scrabbled against stone, pushing it in little circles.

"What happened to *following* it?" Yoshi asked.

"It was stealing the device. We can't climb back down in normal G." Anna pulled the flashlight from the motionless whiskers and shined it at the smashed robot's remains. "Besides, there's some interesting stuff in here."

She pried one of the pieces loose—a black rectangle about the size of a pack of cards. "This is really warm. It could be a battery."

"Fascinating." Yoshi sighed. "But I wish you hadn't—"

"Shh!" Kira hissed, and pointed her flashlight into the depths of the cave.

Two more machines were scuttling forward from the shadows, their whiskers waving furiously.

"Do they look angry to you?" Yoshi asked.

"Not at all. My guess is they're programmed to ignore us." Anna dropped the battery into her backpack. "Think about it. This whole place is a giant biology experiment. So these robots must be designed not to mess with animals."

Yoshi wasn't sure he liked being called an animal, but Anna's theory seemed to hold—the robots ignored the three of them, scuttling forward to check on their damaged fellow machine. Their whiskers wrapped around it, and they began to drag it laboriously back into the darkness.

Anna pulled a bungee cord from her backpack and crept after them. She clipped one end of the cord to the wounded robot.

"Okay," Anna said. "*Now* we follow them."

Yoshi slipped his scabbard over his shoulder and readied his flashlight. Who knew what they were going to find back there?

Just then a cool breeze drifted across the back of his neck, and Yoshi smelled something oily and sharp.

He turned back toward the cave entrance. The night wind must have carried the huge pillar of smoke toward them, along with the scent of burning aircraft. He recognized the jet-fuel smell, and another like burned plastic.

What if the others were already dead?

30

Anna

Anna was jealous of the robots.

Their eight legs were separately articulated, designed perfectly for scuttling across uneven rock. And they were small enough to stroll down claustrophobic tunnels where Anna and the others had to take off their backpacks to squeeze through.

The machines would've lost her within minutes, except for the bungee cord. She used it like a leash, pulling back the broken robot every time it got too far ahead. When she gave it a tug the other robots would lose their grip, then come back and investigate. Sometimes they would detach the bungee cord, but Anna simply clipped it on again.

They weren't very *smart* robots. But their behavior made perfect sense if this jungle really was artificial. They were programmed to ignore anything living, to interact only with other machines. In other words, they were *maintenance* robots, which was why they'd tried to steal Kira's flashlight and the gravity device.

Whatever they were, following them had to lead to whoever had designed all this. Someone who could create this kind of technology could definitely help Molly.

"You guys okay back there?" Anna asked.

Yoshi answered with an exhausted grunt.

Anna couldn't blame him. Crawling through these tunnels was tiring, especially after a day of jumping and that endless climb. Her muscles were rubbery, her jacket drenched in sweat. The rocks around them seemed to grow hotter as they went deeper into the mountain.

But none of that discomfort was enough to drown out the numbness in Anna's heart.

The airplane had burned up so suddenly, like a giant firebomb, so fast that if anyone had been asleep inside, they wouldn't have escaped—

Jet fuel burned at about a thousand degrees. Hot enough to reduce a human body to ashes and shards of bone.

Anna shook off the thought and kept crawling. The only way to help her friends was to find whoever had made these robots.

There was something ahead, a shift in the color of the rocks.

"Turn off the flashlights," she whispered.

Yoshi repeated the command in Japanese, and a moment later Anna was in darkness. It took a moment for her eyes to adjust, then she saw it clearly—an orange glow just ahead.

Maybe it was bioluminescence, just a colony of glow-worms. Of course, if the glowworms in this place were like everything else, there would be no "just" about it.

Kira said something, and Yoshi translated, "Do you hear that?"

Anna listened, and a soft fluttering sound filled the air. Like the wings of a flock of pigeons, or cards being shuffled in some large, echoey space.

The bungee cord went slack.

A she crawled ahead, the passage widened and the orange glow grew brighter. Anna saw more machines gathered around the broken robot. It was being dismantled, the pieces carried away.

Yep. Maintenance robots, scavenging for spare parts.

She reeled the bungee cord back in and shoved it in her pocket.

"I think we're here," she said. "Wherever here is."

The tunnel opened up into a huge cavern, the size of the gymnasium back at Brooklyn Science and Tech. Inset into the stone walls were countless orange lights, all of them dancing on and off. It was hot, like a Laundromat in midsummer, but cool drafts spilled from another dozen passages leading away into the rock.

Across the floor scuttled dozens of the eight-legged machines. They carried pieces of metal and clusters of fiber, and navigated around Anna's feet without hesitation or interest.

"Hello?" she called. Her voice echoed, but no answer came except the fluttering sound of the blinking lights.

"*Omoshiroi ne,*" Kira said, crossing to the center of the cavern.

Floating there was some kind of display, a hologram or a model. One end of it seemed to represent the jungle, familiar from the view they'd seen out of the mouth of the cave.

As Anna went closer, she saw that the rest of the model represented a long, ragged valley, a rift carved into the earth. The rift was bordered by high stone walls on either side, and tiny waterfalls poured from the rocks—the model was *moving.*

Near the center of the jungle was a glowing fire, the crashed airplane rendered in perfect resolution, not even an inch long. The two artificial moons hovered a foot above the trees, glowing red and green.

"Whoa," she said.

Kira stood on the other side of the display, already drawing.

"It's a machine," Yoshi said.

Anna nodded. "Some kind of hologram, maybe."

"No, I mean it's *all one big machine.*" He pointed at the display. "The jungle is held in by these walls. The waterfalls and mists pour down to keep it wet. Every bit of it is artificial."

"Sure." Anna narrowed her eyes. "But if this is all a machine, what's its purpose?"

"To maintain the jungle?"

"Um, jungles maintain themselves. It takes a *lot* of effort to kill them."

Yoshi shrugged. "That depends on what's behind this wall."

Anna peered closer at the model. It only extended to the walls of rock and didn't show what was on the other side. Farther down its length, the red and green of trees faded into other colors—beige, ochre, a few bands of glimmering silver. They weren't as high resolution as the jungle, but each looked like it was some different kind of terrain.

Anna reached out and touched the display. It wasn't a hologram at all—it was really there, but it felt as soft as cotton candy.

Some kind of aerogel? That *moved*?

The display also pulsed and shivered with data—swirls of color hovered over the crashed airplane, flashing angrily.

Kira said something, and Yoshi translated. "She says this place was built for dozens of people to work in."

Anna nodded. The smooth expanse of rock overhead was at least twelve feet high, but the little robots only needed a few inches of clearance. She imagined people standing around the display, reading the mysterious graphics, drawing their plans for the jungle below.

But where were they now?

The cavern suddenly felt empty and haunted. Like the crashed airplane after the passengers had disappeared. Nothing left but mindless machines.

No one to help with Molly's sickness.

"Is anybody *here*?" she yelled out.

No answer.

"Maybe it's all automatic," Yoshi said tiredly.

"Then who's this display *for*?" Anna demanded. "The robots don't need it. I'm not even sure they have eyes!"

One of the little machines was nuzzling her foot, and Anna felt a rush of anger at its mindless skittering, at all these signs of civilization that had promised help for Molly but now offered *nothing*.

The robot extended a whisker, reaching up for her backpack. Anna gave it a swift kick, and it clattered away across the stone.

"Um," Yoshi said. "Maybe you shouldn't do that."

Anna didn't answer him—the other end of the model had caught her eye. There, opposite the jungle, was some kind of structure. It was as big as a dinner plate, ten times larger than the tiny crashed airplane. Kira stood at that end already, drawing it.

Anna went to take a closer look.

It was covered with spires that stuck out in all directions—a madhouse version of a castle, or maybe a futuristic city. The structure's core gave off a soft red glow, pulsing like a heartbeat.

Whatever it was, there had to be someone there.

People with answers. People who could help Molly.

Anna pointed at the structure. "This looks like the headquarters for whoever built all this. We have to get there!"

Yoshi looked down the length of the model, then back at the jungle.

"That seems pretty far."

"But we have to *try*," Anna said, but he was right. The hologram stretched endlessly down the cavern. A panic started to build in her, the feeling that no matter what they did, they would be too late. "Maybe we should look around. Find something that might help Molly."

"Okay," Yoshi said. "But what are we looking for?"

"Anything!" Anna glared at the little robots underfoot. Most of them carried spare parts, pieces of metal and wire and plastic. Something had to be worth plundering.

She crushed one of the passing robots underfoot.

"Anna," Yoshi pleaded. "Be careful."

"They're just repair bots," she said. "They don't even see us."

He opened his mouth to argue, but suddenly his expression changed. He was staring over her shoulder, frozen.

Anna followed his gaze—at the opening of one of the passages was a new kind of machine, much larger than the little robots. It hunkered in a menacing crouch, its four legs and two arms folded around it, each ending in large, sharp-looking pincers.

"Uh-oh," Kira said.

The machine rose up, its arms waving, their pincers snapping like metal jaws, and cold fear swept through Anna.

Yoshi took a step backward. "What on earth is that?"

Anna swallowed.

"I think it's animal control," she said. "And we're the animals."

Yoshi

Anna turned and ran, heading for the nearest open passageway.

Yoshi followed, grabbing Kira by the arm as he flew past. He flicked on the flashlight in his free hand.

The passage had a low ceiling, forcing him to stoop as he ran. The clatter of metal feet echoed behind him.

"See?" he cried. "Kicking those little robots wasn't smart!"

Anna looked back. "It was trying to take my stuff!"

Yoshi didn't bother arguing. Kira already had a good lead on them, her size making it easier to run in the cramped tunnel.

The animal control machine—or whatever it was— clattered along only a few yards behind Yoshi. He wondered if it was equipped with nets, or tranquilizer darts, or something more lethal. He doubted his sword could do anything to its metal limbs.

But at the moment, at least, the robot seemed content to scare them away. Maybe it really did think they were animals.

If he stopped running and faced it, would the machine even know what to do? Maybe it would just give up.

On the other hand, maybe those metal pincers would slice his head off.

Yoshi kept running.

"Find a narrow tunnel!" Kira called back to them. "Somewhere that thing can't fit!"

"She thinks we can hide," he translated. "Somewhere small."

"It's too close!" Anna panted.

They went skidding around a corner, and suddenly Yoshi's feet were crashing through a mob of little eight-legged robots, all of them loaded with cargoes of mechanical parts.

Yoshi tried to jump them, but his foot struck metal and he flew forward. The flashlight slipped from his hand, cracked against stone, then went spinning away. The hard floor rushed up and met his right knee. A spark of pain knocked his breath away, and a moment later he was rolling to a halt across the rocky floor.

The larger robot bore down on him, its pincers gleaming in the dark, and Yoshi covered his head—

But the machine jumped, sailing over him, and kept going, snatching up the flashlight on its way.

"Huh," Yoshi said, wincing with pain as he stood.

The robot didn't care about him, just his flashlight. That was good news, except for one thing—it would take the gravity device away.

Which was their only way of escaping the mountain.

Yoshi started to run again, following the sound of the machine down the dark tunnel. There were no flickering orange lights here, just the glimmer of Kira's flashlight ahead. He had to keep one hand on the stone wall to guide himself, and every step sent pain stabbing through his knee.

His feet struck more of the little robots, and he kept stumbling in the darkness. But at last Yoshi felt a breeze against his face and smelled fresh air.

He rounded the next corner and found himself facing an opening in the stone—starlight glittered through it!

Framed against the night sky were Anna, Kira, and the machine. Kira swung her flashlight at the robot, and the clang of metal against metal echoed down the tunnel. Pincers flashed and snapped.

Full of sudden anger, Yoshi charged, running headlong down the tunnel. His sword might be useless, but sometimes brute force was called for—he lowered his shoulder and threw all his weight against the machine.

It was like running straight into motorcycle—the machine was harder and heavier than Yoshi, and pain surged through his whole body. But the metal feet scraped against stone as his momentum carried both him and the robot toward the ledge.

"Yoshi!" Kira cried, reaching out.

The machine's feet scrabbled for purchase, and its pincers grabbed at the ledge as Yoshi gave one last shove.

The robot toppled, its limbs flailing, but Yoshi's momentum carried him after it. The misty abyss opened up beneath him—

Kira's hand grasped his, and for a moment Yoshi was suspended over the endless drop. The muscles in his hands still screamed from the climb, but his fear of falling into the void kept them locked around Kira's fingers.

A moment later, Anna had pulled them both back onto the ledge, and they all collapsed together on the stone.

Yoshi stared at the others, opening his mouth to thank them.

"It's still there!" Kira yelled, pointing.

Hooked to the ledge of the opening was a single pincer, glistening in the starlight.

Yoshi drew back his foot and kicked at it, but his running shoe bounced from the metal, which didn't budge.

Another pincer rose up beside the first, grasping the stone.

"Ready for heavy!" Anna cried, her hands on the gravity device.

Yoshi braced himself, and a moment later the crushing burden of double G fell hard upon him. The pain in his knee spiked, squeezing a grunt from his lungs.

He fought to turn his head and watched the pincers losing their shape, the metal bending under the doubled weight of the robot hanging from them.

Then a vast, strange sound came from everywhere at once—the stone around the cave mouth creaked and shifted. Yoshi wondered how many tons had suddenly been added to the load of rock overhead, weighing down on the passages and caverns that hollowed out the mountain. Dust silted down, a groan passing through the cave mouth.

Then, all at once, the pincers failed, disappearing with a flash of metal. The last frantic scrapings of the robot trying to save itself slid out of Yoshi's hearing.

Anna switched off the device. The weight lifted from Yoshi, and a great wracking breath filled his lungs. The red spots crowding his vision began to disappear.

"You okay?" Kira asked.

Yoshi looked down at himself. His pants were torn, and blood seeped from his knee. When he moved that leg, spikes of pain went through him, but the muscles seemed to be in working order.

"I'll live," he said, but then another groan passed through the stone, the rock shifting unhappily overhead.

Kira raised an eyebrow. "Don't speak too soon."

Anna stood and placed her hand against the stone wall.

"The doubled weight unsettled all these tunnels," she said. "Should I turn the gravity to low?"

Yoshi stared at her. "You're the engineer, not me!"

Anna opened her mouth to say something, but the groaning of the stones around them was growing louder, building to a roar. A sudden darkness shut out the night sky, as if a curtain had fallen across the opening.

Kira pointed her flashlight at it—a torrent of white was streaming past.

"Snow," she said. "We set off an avalanche!"

The snow kept coming, gushing past, and whirlwinds of fluffy powder drifted into the opening. It settled over Yoshi in a cold layer.

But gradually the shifting weight of the avalanche seemed to settle the stone around them. The mountain's groaning eased, fading into the *shush* of falling snow.

Long moments later it tapered off, and the night sky glittered through the cave mouth again.

"Check this out," Anna said, lifting her backpack. It was wet, the snow on it melted. She pulled out the battery she'd stolen from the first little robot. "Still warm. We can use it as a heater, I guess."

Yoshi didn't answer. He scooped his palm across the stone, gathering a handful of the snow and squeezing it into a tiny snowball. It was perfect snow for skiing, he noticed—crystalline, cold, dry powder.

Of course it was.

He looked up at the stars, which sparkled bright in the sky now that the smoke from the distant aircraft fire had cleared.

And he saw it—what Caleb must have seen.

"Ursa," Yoshi said. "He was trying to say Ursa Major."

Anna stood next to him, looking up at the Big Dipper filling the sky.

"It looks exactly the same as at home," she said, pointing. "And look. The North Star is up there, right overhead."

"I hear something," Kira said. "There's more of those big robots coming!"

"We have to jump," Yoshi translated for Anna.

"Okay." She hefted the device, then looked down at the battery in her hand. "We're going to need this heater, aren't we?"

Yoshi nodded. Suddenly, it was all clear.

He knew exactly where they were.

32

Javi

How's she doing?" Oliver asked again.

Javi looked up tiredly and tried to sound more certain than he felt.

"She'll be fine."

Oliver looked away, his lips pressed tight together. Not believing.

Molly hadn't opened her eyes since fainting after the engine fire. Her breathing had been fast and shallow all night, and she was covered with a sheen of sweat. When Javi dribbled water between her lips, she would swallow a few drops and murmur meaningless words, but that was the only sign of consciousness.

The illness seemed to be consuming her. Her face was gaunt, and her muscles and veins stood out on her already wiry limbs.

Worst of all, the wound on her shoulder still glowed that awful, luminous green.

At dawn, Akiko had lured two fat slide-whistle birds straight into Javi's net, and they had a pile of red berries ready, but there was no way to get Molly to eat.

Oliver stood there, waiting for more, and Javi wondered if he wanted the truth. The kid had fought hard to make them all stop sugarcoating things. Maybe it was time to talk to him straight.

"I don't know how she is, but I'm worried," Javi said.

"Then what do we do if the others don't come back?" Oliver asked.

Javi just stared at him.

"We said we'd go look for them after three days."

"Oh, right." Javi looked at Molly, laid out on their remaining airplane blanket. The idea that she could travel in two days seemed ridiculous. "We can't leave her."

"But they'll run out of food!" Oliver persisted.

"They know which berries to eat."

Oliver didn't look satisfied.

Akiko came through the trees, bringing more water. When the fire had been at its hottest the night before, they'd carried Molly away from the airplane and closer to the stream. One flash of smart thinking in a night of terrible decisions.

The mistakes kept echoing through Javi's head. Why use the device on settings they didn't understand? Why experiment on the aircraft itself? Since when was messing with the laws of nature *ever* a good idea?

Javi stared at what was left of the plane. Their only shelter, their only connection with Earth, and they'd burned it to the ground. Most of the equipment they'd painstakingly collected had been incinerated, along with everything they could have scavenged from the hundreds of pieces of luggage they hadn't even opened yet.

The whole camp smelled like a disaster area. Javi's lungs were scorched and his skin was coated with smoke. The surrounding trees were white with ash, and if the dreadful duck appeared again, they had no place left to hide.

Akiko knelt to dribble some water into Molly's mouth, and Javi stood up to stretch, trying to breathe deep enough to clear his mind of awful thoughts.

"She won't die, will she?" Oliver asked softly.

Maybe he didn't want the truth after all.

Javi shook his head, and not just for Oliver's sake.

Molly *couldn't* die.

Without her, they weren't a team anymore. Without her, they had no leader, no one to challenge them to find solutions in this strange place. It was bad enough, the thought that they might never get home.

But to lose Molly as well . . .

The explorers came back that night, a day early.

They must have seen the signal fire, which Akiko and Oliver had built to help guide them home. The three of them came skimming in just as the sun was setting, bounding over sliced-off trees in the landing path.

As they descended, Javi felt the low-gravity field of their device lift his tired muscles for a moment. The bonfire ruffled and sparked, then settled again as normal weight returned. Akiko and Kira ran to embrace each other, spinning off into their own private stream of French and Japanese.

"Are you okay?" Oliver said. He was staring at Yoshi, whose knee was wrapped up in a bloody bungee cord.

"I'm fine," came Yoshi's answer. But he looked pale, and he walked toward the fire with a definite limp.

"He had an argument with a robot," Anna said.

Yoshi half shrugged. "Which I won."

They looked exhausted, and when Anna spotted the slide-whistle bird plucked and ready by the fire, her eyes went wide.

"Wait," Javi said. "Did you just say a *robot*? Does that mean you found *people*?"

Yoshi started to answer, but then he saw the form stretched out in the shadows beyond the fire. "Is that Molly?"

Javi nodded. "She's worse. Um, we kind of blew up the plane."

"We saw," Anna said blankly.

A moment later all six of them were crowded around Molly's unconscious form, and Javi was explaining everything—how they'd found the two new settings, set the airplane on fire, and barely escaped being burned to death. And how Molly had fainted after all the excitement.

"She hasn't moved since," he finished. "I don't know what to do."

"We can get her help," Anna said.

Oliver looked up. "So you did find people?"

"No." Anna took a breath. "But someone *made* this jungle, and we think we know where they are."

Javi blinked, his brain too tired to understand.

"Wait. We're on Earth?" he managed.

"We're exactly where we're supposed to be," Yoshi said. "Behind the waterfall was a huge wall of stone, maybe miles high. Someone built it. Someone built *all* of this."

"The wall's full of machines," Anna said. "Tons of weird technology, along with robots that maintain it. The whole thing is wrapped around this valley, to protect it."

Javi stared at them. They looked tired, but not like they'd gone crazy in the last two days. And he'd seen plenty of stranger things than robots and giant walls since the crash.

"Protect it from what?"

"The arctic," Yoshi said simply.

"We were almost at the top of the wall," Anna explained. "And when we doubled the gravity, a ton of snow came tumbling down. We triggered an avalanche, because our plane crashed exactly where it should have—somewhere not that far from the North Pole."

"We even saw the Big Dipper." Yoshi looked up. "Also known as Ursa Major. That's what Caleb was trying to tell us."

"The walls are heated, to keep the jungle warm," Anna said. "The water comes from melted snow, and the mist covers everything because it's way hotter down here than the tundra around us."

"Down here?" Javi asked.

"We're down in a valley, a rift in the earth." Yoshi said something to Kira, who brought over her drawing pad. "We saw a model of the whole thing. The jungle's at one end, and some kind of huge building is at the other, with a lot of other stuff between."

Javi stared at the drawing—some strange futuristic castle. "But why would anyone build a whole valley in the arctic? And such a *weird* one?"

"Good question," Anna said. "But whoever it was, they must know how to help Molly. If they designed all this, they can fix whatever poison that bird left in her."

Javi could only nod at this. If it would save Molly, he was willing to believe anything. "So how do we contact them?"

"They don't answer the radio, and there was no one in the wall," Anna said. "So we have to go to the other end of the rift."

"It's that way." Yoshi pointed toward the front of the plane.

Javi sat down heavily, staring into Molly's still face. For a moment, he'd thought they were all saved. That it was simply a matter of sending out a distress call and waiting for rescue parties to show up.

"How are we supposed to get there?" he asked. "She can't walk."

Molly's eyes fluttered open.

"Simple," she said. "We fly."

33

Molly

Molly recognized the voices, but it took a long time to understand the words flowing over her. They'd sounded like an alien language at first, or the gabbling of birds. But finally their meaning had trickled into her brain.

She'd listened and realized that Anna and Yoshi were only half right—this *was* a valley, a rift in the arctic snows. But it was also a rift in the world itself, and somehow Molly had fallen deeper into it than the others.

She had to wake up now, or she never would.

Molly sat up slowly, looking into each of the startled faces around her.

She could see them all clearly now. Yoshi was battered, exhausted, but a new determination surged in him, now that he had a goal. Javi was filled with relief, ready to do as she commanded. Anna was still walled off. She'd never really faced the airplane crash or the numbness that threatened to swallow her. Oliver and Akiko looked like they were about to cry—they were still themselves after everything that had happened.

Kira was calmly staring at Molly, studying her, reaching for her pencils. She was the only one who saw the change.

The air smelled different now, full of a million weird scents Molly hadn't noticed before. It was too much, like someone was trying to cram a thousand new sensations into her mind.

Her shoulder burned, and she still felt faint. She tried to swallow away the acid taste in her mouth.

Javi gave her a handful of blue berries. They tasted wrong, cloying and soapy. Molly dropped them to the ground and reached for the red *omoshiroi*-berries instead. They were sweet and delicious, full of everything her body needed.

Red was good.

It was green you had to watch out for.

Molly saw it now—pukeberries, shredder birds, the baleful smaller moon that signaled danger. And of course the dreadful duck of doom.

Stay away from green.

"Are you okay?" Javi asked gently.

Molly nodded. Maybe *okay* was the wrong word, but she was *something*.

"I'll be ready to go soon," she said. "We should start right away."

Javi frowned. "Start what?"

"Looking for answers."

They all stared at her.

"We have to find out what crashed our plane," she said. "Why we survived when no one else did."

"Okay," Javi said. "How?"

"Same as always," she said. "We gather data. We form conclusions. We figure this out." She swallowed some water. Water, at least, tasted exactly the same. "I think we're here for a reason. I think the answers are at the other end of the rift."

She'd seen it on the plane, in her dream before the crash, the thing in the distance—something powerful and dangerous. Something acting with intention.

Each of them had been chosen. She was sure of it. The electricity that had moved through the cabin had picked them all with deadly purpose.

"Molly's right," Yoshi said. "The other end of the rift is the only way out. We could climb the walls with low gravity, but we'd never make it across the arctic."

"And there's no point sticking around here," Anna added, gesturing at the burned-out plane. "For one thing, we stirred up those robots back at the wall, and they might have followed us."

Javi gave a tired sigh. "I just wish you guys had seen the first-class cabin. It was baller."

Yoshi started translating for Akiko and Kira, but the girls seemed to have understood already. Everyone was ready to move on, to go wherever the promise of answers lay.

Molly wanted to sink back onto the pile of cushions, to sleep and dream some more. To prepare herself. But there had to be new dangers moving toward them even now. The catastrophic airplane fire was too big a wound for the jungle to ignore.

It would be a long journey, longer than the others were ready to understand yet. She was going to have to carry them at least part of the way, when they lost hope and nothing made sense.

But that was okay. Molly Davis had been born to lead.

She was different now, but she was still herself.

And she would get them home.

ABOUT THE AUTHOR

Scott Westerfeld is the #1 *New York Times* bestselling author of the Uglies series, which has been translated into thirty-five languages; the Leviathan series; the Zeroes series (cowritten with Margo Lanagan and Deborah Biancotti); *Afterworlds*; and many other books for young readers. He was born in Texas, and alternates summers between Sydney, Australia, and New York City.

THE GAME

A small group of survivors steps from
the wreckage of a plane . . .
And you're one of them.

JOIN THE RACE FOR SURVIVAL!

1. Download the app or go to **scholastic.com/horizon**
2. Log in to create your character.
3. Go to the Sequencer in your home camp.
4. Input the above musical sequence.
5. Claim your prize!

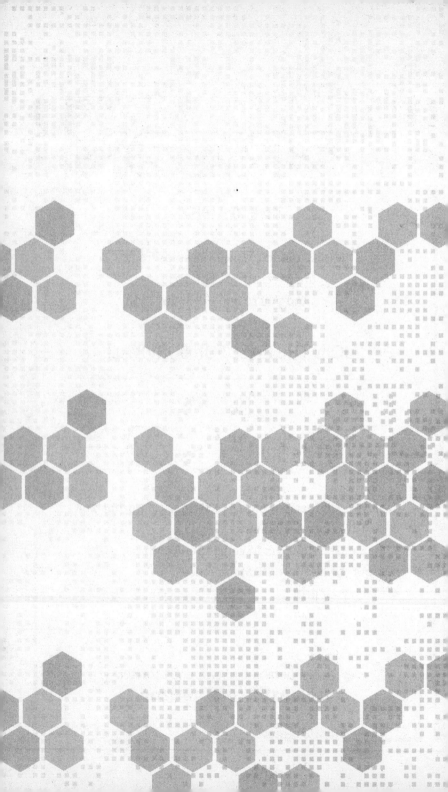